Hannah's lips fo... ...couldn't summo... ...Her chest ached ... ...down on it like a ...

She'd dreamed of him so often, with fondness and fury, and there he was. His presence seemed to fill the sanctuary from carpet to rafters. She'd tried so hard to forget those eyes, and there they were, staring back at her with that same unnerving intensity.

What was he doing here? What did he want? Why now? Why ever? What was she supposed to do about Rebecca?

He expected her to say something; she knew that. The words just wouldn't come. Words couldn't squeeze past the guilt clawing at her insides. No matter what he'd done, no matter how hurt she'd felt, she should have found a way to tell him as soon as she knew. Or at least she could have found some occasion before Rebecca's fourth birthday. What was she supposed to tell him now?

Books by Dana Corbit

Love Inspired

A Blessed Life
An Honest Life
A New Life
A Family for Christmas
  "Child in a Manger"
On the Doorstep
Christmas in the Air
  "Season of Hope"
A Hickory Ridge Christmas
Little Miss Matchmaker
Homecoming at Hickory Ridge
*An Unexpected Match
*His Christmas Bride
*Wedding Cake Wishes
Safe in His Arms

*Wedding Bell Blessings

DANA CORBIT

started telling "people stories" at about the same time she started forming words. So it came as no surprise when the Indiana native chose a career in journalism. As an award-winning newspaper reporter and features editor, she had the opportunity to share wonderful true-life stories with her readers. She left the workforce to be a homemaker, but the stories came home with her as she discovered the joy of writing fiction. The winner of the 2007 Holt Medallion competition for novel writing, Dana feels blessed to share the stories of her heart with readers.

Dana lives in southeast Michigan, where she balances the make-believe realm of her characters with her equally exciting real-life world as a wife, carpool coordinator for three athletic daughters and food supplier for two uninterested felines.

A Hickory Ridge Christmas

Dana Corbit

Love Inspired

Recycling programs
for this product may
not exist in your area.

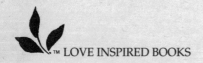

™ LOVE INSPIRED BOOKS

ISBN-13: 978-0-373-78732-6

A HICKORY RIDGE CHRISTMAS

Printed in U.S.A.

And be kind to one another, tenderhearted,
forgiving one another,
as God in Christ forgave you.
                    —*Ephesians* 4:32

To our firstborn daughter, Marissa, who has been asking me to write Hannah and Todd's story for four years now. You already have so many wonderful stories in you. I hope you find joy in telling them.

A special thanks to Monsignor John Budde for his biblical research assistance; Michael G. Thomas, C.P.A., for his knowledge of the accounting field; and, as always, to my favorite medical expert, Dr. Celia D'Errico, D.O.

Chapter One

For the third time in as many weeks, Hannah Woods awoke smiling. She wasn't fully awake. Not really. For if she were, then the practical side of her mind would have insisted that she rein in those banned images. She was far too busy and far too focused to entertain little-girl dreams, at least in her conscious hours. She hadn't been a little girl for a very long time.

Just this once, though, in that private place between slumber and alertness, Hannah couldn't resist the temptation to let those pictures play out in full color.

Keeping her eyes tightly closed, Hannah let herself glance around in her make-believe world and take in sights and sounds so real that she could almost hear the organ prelude and smell sweet roses and pooling candle wax. Her heart warmed at the sight of her father standing at the altar, his Bible open to a familiar passage.

She couldn't picture herself, but she could almost feel tulle brushing her cheek and lacy bridal point, making her wrists itch. The last image, though, made her breath catch in her throat. Todd. Always Todd.

Standing across the aisle from her, he looked so handsome in his dark tuxedo. His shoulders had filled out the way she'd always imagined they would someday, but he still had the same boy's face she remembered, and his green eyes were as mesmerizing as ever. Those eyes still looked as sincere as they had when he'd told her he loved her.

When he'd lied.

As Hannah came fully awake with a start and sat straight up in bed, the twinkling lights of the miniature Christmas tree shifted into focus. They'd set it up the day before while still digesting their Thanksgiving turkey. This morning the tree's tinsel, garland and tiny red bows replaced all satin and pastel thoughts of the wedding that would never be.

What was she doing, anyway? She didn't have the luxury of indulging useless, adolescent dreams. And if she continued forgetting to unplug that little tree at night, especially with the apartment's wiring, they would be sifting through charred rubble before New Year's.

Clearly, she needed to get her act together. She was twenty-two years old now, not seventeen. She had responsibilities and obligations—things Todd knew nothing about and probably couldn't have handled if he knew. *You never gave him the chance to handle anything,* an unwelcome voice inside her pointed out with a punch she did her best to dodge. Forgiveness.

She'd given that the old college try these past five years, but she couldn't quite get beyond the desertion part. Whether or not it had been his choice to leave with his parents when his father had been transferred to Singapore, the fact remained that he *had* left when she'd needed him most.

Perhaps only God could forgive and truly *forget*.

A litany of her own sins and failures played in her mind as it always did when her thoughts turned to the boy she should have forgotten—the boy who was now a man. She would have allowed guilt to blanket her as she had so many times while the months stretched into years, but the squeak of her bedroom door offered a reprieve this time.

"I'm awake, Mommy," Rebecca called out as she bounded into the room, tucked something under the bed and then scrambled on top of the covers.

Though her child made that same announcement and followed the same routine every morning at about ten minutes before the alarm was set to go off, Hannah smiled. "Well, looky there. I guess you are."

"Is it Friday? Do I have my playdate with Max today?"

"Yes, sweetie, it's today."

Since Rebecca had been counting down the days until her playdate with her favorite friend, Max Williams, Hannah was pleased to finally say yes. Technically, the "playdate" was really only a day when Mary Nelson would be babysitting both Rebecca and Max while Hannah worked at the accounting firm and while Max's mother, Tricia Williams Lancaster, scoured Twelve Oaks Mall on the busiest shopping day of the year. Hannah didn't bother clarifying the point.

"Today. Today. Today!" Rebecca threw her head back on the bed and wiggled with the type of delight only a child could find before breakfast without a double espresso. Her fine towhead-blond hair stuck up every which way, and she squeezed her eyes shut tight, probably looking for the stars she liked to watch behind her eyelids.

Reaching down, Hannah brushed the hair back from her daughter's fair-skinned face, all thoughts of obligations flittering away on a wave of pure adoration.

Rebecca opened her eyes and stared up at her mom. Hannah's chest tightened. It was probably the dream that made her react again to her daughter's green eyes when she'd been so proud of her ability to no longer notice them. Others probably hadn't found Rebecca's eye color remarkable since Hannah's eyes were a hazel-green shade—close but not the same. She saw it, though. Those were Todd's eyes that sometimes stared back when her daughter looked at her.

Clearing her throat, she gave the child a tight squeeze. "We'd better get up or we'll be late."

Rebecca lifted her head off the bed, and her bottom lip came out in a pout. "But…"

"Why? Do you have a better idea?"

The little girl pointed to the side of the bed.

"Is there something under there I should know about?"

Lying back and wiggling again, Rebecca nodded.

Hannah pressed her index finger to her lips as if pondering and then glanced down at her. "Is it bigger than a bread box?"

Rebecca's eyebrows furrowed. "What's a bread box?"

"A thing people used to use to keep bread fresh." Hannah gave the same answer she did every day.

"Nope."

"Is it smaller than an amoeba?"

"What's an amoeba?"

"A single-cell creature."

"Nope." A giggle erupted from the child's rosebud mouth. "Do you want to know what it is?"

"You'd better tell me. I just can't guess."

Rebecca climbed off the bed, peered under it and returned with the *surprise:* today's choice from their collection of Christmas storybooks they'd recently taken out of storage.

"Ooh, the manger story!" Hannah accepted the hardcover book, pleased with her daughter's selection with its quotes from the Book of Luke and Michelangelo-style painted illustrations. Hannah enjoyed reading all the festive stories to her daughter, but she was excited that Rebecca had chosen one that spoke of the true Christmas story instead of one about Rudolph and the rest of the holiday gang.

"There's baby Jesus." Rebecca pointed to the book cover, which featured a painting of the sweet infant, a halo of glory about his head. "And the sheep and the cows and the donkey."

"Looks like they're all there." Hannah opened the book to the first page, and Rebecca snuggled up under her arm. Only after they'd read the last page could they officially begin their day.

"The end," Rebecca announced with glee when they were finished.

Again Hannah smiled at her daughter. Rebecca approached everything with that same kind of enthusiasm, as if each hour was an uncharted land just waiting to be explored.

How could Hannah have forgotten, even for a minute, how fortunate she was to know this amazing four-year-old? How grateful she was to God for giving her the privilege of raising her. Loving Rebecca had nothing to do with obligation and so much to do with sharing in the joy and in the discovery.

During her conscious hours, Hannah didn't give herself time for regrets, not when she and Rebecca enjoyed so many blessings. If only she could rein in the images that crowded her dreams, as well. Those snapshots of the past hurt more than they healed, leaving her to awaken feeling empty and wondering whether something vital was missing from her life.

Todd took a deep breath as he stepped inside the church's glass double doors Sunday morning. If only he could remove the golf-ball-sized knot clogging his throat. He felt as queasy as an actor on opening night, only this wasn't a play and the only reviewer who mattered was sure to give him a scorching review.

Before he could even stomp the snow off his dress shoes and hang his coat on the rack that extended the length of the vestibule, an usher approached him.

"Welcome to Hickory Ridge Community Church," the man said as he gripped Todd's hand and pumped briskly. "Is this your first time visiting with us?"

Clearing his throat, Todd answered, "No—I mean it's been a long time, but—" he coughed into his hand and looked back up at the usher "—it isn't my first time."

"And we sure hope it won't be the last."

Todd tilted his head to indicate the crowded sanctuary, visible through a wall of windows. "I'd better get in there. I'm already late."

The man brushed away the comment with a wave of his hand. "Ah, they're just getting warmed up in there."

Todd thanked the man and continued past him. He'd hoped that arriving after services started would allow him to miss a formal greeting at the door, but he should have known better. Hickory Ridge had always been a friendly church on the "Bring-A-Friend Sunday" and the "Homecoming" events he'd attended with Hannah, and clearly that hadn't changed.

Plenty of other things were just as familiar, he found, as he peered through the windows into the sanctuary. Same stained glass window behind the choir loft. Same red carpet and red-padded pews. Same crowd of strangers. Same two guys sitting on the twin benches on either side of the pulpit.

Only the draped garland in the front of the sanctuary and the candles in the sills of the other stained glass windows even hinted at how long it had been since he'd visited. Those things suggested that months and seasons had sped by, but that mammoth second building behind the church where a field had once been, announced the passing of years.

The years scared him most of all.

Now that he was twenty-two, maybe it was too late. Maybe it had always been too late, and he'd only been deceiving himself, balancing on a tenuous lie of hope. The messages contained in airmail letters marked Returned To Sender and in the clicks of hang-ups for international calls should have been enough to convince him, but he'd refused to take the hints.

With his hand pressed on the door separating the vestibule from the sanctuary, he hesitated. His chest felt so tight that it ached to breathe. How could he move forward when it felt as if every moment of his life for half a decade had led him to this point?

How could he not?

Straightening his shoulders, he swung open the door and followed its path into the sanctuary. He slipped into the third pew from the back just as a music leader asked everyone to stand. Even as he turned pages in his hymnal, Todd couldn't help scanning the sea of heads. Where was she? Would he recognize her now? Even though he had it on good authority that she still attended

Hickory Ridge, it didn't mean she wouldn't be sick this morning or out of town for Thanksgiving weekend.

Soon strains of "Just a Closer Walk With Thee" swirled around him, its lyrics celebrating the promise of God's presence. Warmth spread inside him, relieving some of the tightness in his chest. It was just like his God to find a way to remind him He was there, even when Todd was too preoccupied to sing the words.

As the song ended and the congregation sat, youth minister Andrew Westin stepped to the lectern. "Good morning, everyone, and welcome to Hickory Ridge. I hope you had a wonderful Thanksgiving."

Andrew's gaze settled on Todd, and a smile pulled at his lips. Of course, Andrew had been expecting to see him there. Todd should have known that he hadn't fooled anyone with his veiled questions when he'd called the church office a few days before. Especially not Andrew Westin. The Harley-riding youth minister never had struck Todd as any kind of fool.

As if Andrew recognized the question in Todd's eyes, he turned his head and directed his gaze toward a group of young adults sitting on the second pew. A couple of people on one end, a fancily dressed middle-aged woman on the other, and there she sat in the middle.

Todd didn't know if the world stopped turning or if time hiccuped, but for a few seconds or minutes, everything beyond her ceased to exist.

Even from behind that crowd of blondes, brunettes and silver-haired ladies, he couldn't imagine how he'd missed her before. He should have recognized that long, light blond ponytail anywhere, as it flowed down the back of her simple peach sweater. Hannah had often worn her hair just that way—smooth, neat and without fuss—and it was the feminine style he still found most attractive.

A piano introduction pulled Todd from his daze, but he couldn't wrap his thoughts around the words or the message of the second hymn. It shouldn't have surprised him. He'd always had tunnel vision when it came to Hannah, and that apparently hadn't changed. He couldn't remember a time when he didn't love her, and he couldn't imagine a future when he would be able to or even want to stop.

Around Hannah, Todd studied the group of young adults in her row and the one behind it, but none of them looked familiar. A tall, light-haired guy shared a hymnal with Hannah, but Todd couldn't remember seeing him, either, during his handful of visits. A few people were paying attention to the hymn, anyway. Todd was far too busy craning his neck and trying to get a glimpse of Hannah's face.

When the song ended, Reverend Bob Woods, who had grayed the last few years and now wore glasses, stepped to the lectern. He scanned the congregation, hesitating only briefly when he reached Todd. The minister's expression didn't change, but his Adam's apple bobbed. Guilt had Todd shifting in his seat.

Just because Hannah's father recognized him didn't automatically mean she'd confided in him about humiliating past events. Todd hadn't changed that much since they were next-door neighbors—at least, not on the outside. Anyway, it couldn't make any difference what Reverend Bob or Andrew Westin or anyone else knew about mistakes they'd made when they were still teenagers. He was here to make amends no matter what.

For a few seconds, the minister bowed his head as if in prayer, and then he looked up and smiled. "I'd like to add my welcome to Andrew's. We're so glad you're here. Whether you're longtime members or looking for a new church home, we're setting out the welcome mat."

Todd blinked. The minister probably offered that same greeting every Sunday, but this invitation felt more personal than that. For the first time since he'd pulled his car into the church parking lot and prepared for his past to collide with his present, he felt his confidence returning.

He did his best to focus on worship as Reverend Bob delivered a message on the birth of John the Baptist, that had taken place just prior to Jesus's birth, but no matter how hard Todd tried, he couldn't keep his attention from returning to Hannah. He'd waited so long to see her, had imagined this moment for what felt like forever, and here he was waiting again.

Please give me patience, Lord, and give me the words to make things right. Amen.

Hannah turned so that her lovely profile came into view. Her skin still looked as soft as he remembered, but the sprinkling of freckles across her nose appeared to have faded with time. Had her dimples, the tiny ones that only appeared when she really smiled, deepened as she'd entered her twenties? Did her eyes still crinkle at the corners when she laughed? Did those same eyes flood with tears whenever she spoke of her mother?

She tilted her head, appearing engrossed in her father's sermon. Todd hoped she'd had many reasons to smile and to laugh in the years since he'd left. More than anything, he wanted happiness for Hannah, who'd already known so much pain.

If only he could have been a better friend to her, could have provided a strong shoulder and a listening ear, instead of allowing his comforting touch to become something more. No, he hadn't been alone in that bed or alone in his decision to seek passion over purity, but he couldn't help believing he was more responsible than she was. He'd known how fragile Hannah was even so many months after her mom's death. Only one of them had been in any emotional state to put on the brakes in their relationship, and he'd ignored thoughts of sin and regret and gave in to temptation anyway.

He'd known a lot of regret since then.

With effort, Todd set aside the emotions that threatened to distance him from his purpose. He glanced up at her again just as the congregation was singing the last chorus. The blond guy leaned close to Hannah and whispered something in her ear, and though she put her finger to her lips to hush him, her dimples appeared as she chuckled.

Todd's stomach tightened, and for the first time he gave the guy standing next to Hannah more than a passing glance. He'd worked so hard and had planned his return from overseas so carefully. Earning his engineering degree from Nanyang Technological University, targeting his job search to test engineering positions at General Motors Proving Grounds—everything—had been part of this long-term plan to work his way back to her.

He'd thought he'd looked at every obstacle. Clearly, he'd missed a huge one by never considering that Hannah might have dated other guys or even have found someone special in the last five years. Any man would have been crazy not to recognize Hannah for the amazing person she was and consider himself blessed to be with her.

The thought that Hannah might have dated others tore at his heart though he had no right to feel that way. Just because there had never been anyone else for him didn't mean she'd felt the same way.

What was he supposed to do now? No. He shook his head to clear his thoughts. He'd returned to Milford for two reasons only: to apologize to Hannah and to earn her forgiveness. Okay, he'd had secret hopes of building a life with Hannah, but he should have learned by now that he wasn't the type of guy meant for happy endings. Still, he was the type of guy who, just this once, would do the right thing no matter what it cost him.

By the time Todd returned his attention to the front of the church, Andrew had stepped forward to pronounce the benediction.

"Father, lead us as we go out into Your world. Teach us to really love as You love and to forgive as You forgive. In the name of Your Son. Amen." After the prayer, Andrew ascended the aisle, waving at Todd as he passed.

Suddenly, a few things made sense. Was that what Andrew had really meant when he'd said some of the people Todd might know from the youth group had moved away? Had Andrew been referring to Hannah moving on with her life…without him?

Todd steeled himself again. It didn't matter. He couldn't let it matter. He'd waited an awfully long time and gone to more trouble than most men would ever consider to give this apology. Nothing, not even his owns fears, could stop him from doing what he had to do.

With resolve, he looked to the front of the sanctuary, past the other congregants who were chatting and gathering their coats. At first, he thought he'd missed her and that she'd left by one of the side aisle doors. Some of the people she'd been sitting with, including the blond guy, were already gone. But then she straightened from where she'd bent to retrieve her Bible.

Hannah turned her head to say something to the woman next to her, and then she stopped. He knew the minute she recognized him because her eyes widened, and her lovely mouth went slack.

For several seconds, neither moved. Todd felt like a spectator to his own life, unable to look away while the one woman he'd ever loved stared back at him as if he was the last person she ever expected to see again. Or maybe ever wanted to see.

As the Bible she held slipped from her fingers, its pages fluttering open on its path to the floor, Todd felt as if some small part of him—something elemental like hope—died.

Chapter Two

Todd.

Hannah's lips formed the word, but she couldn't summon the breath to give it sound. Her chest ached as fear and panic pressed down on it like a heavy hand.

She'd dreamed of him so often, with fondness and fury, and there he was. His presence seemed to fill the sanctuary from carpet to rafters. She'd tried so hard to forget those eyes, and there they were, staring back at her with that same unnerving intensity.

What was he doing here? What did he want? Why now? Why ever? Rebecca. What was she supposed to do about Rebecca?

Hannah didn't know how long she'd stood there staring or even that she'd dropped her Bible until her friend Steffie Wilmington pressed it back into her sweaty hands. She could barely hold on to its smooth leather cover.

She lowered her gaze to the Bible's gold lettering

and then turned back to the college freshman standing next to her. "Um…thanks."

Remembering where they were and how well attended the Sunday service had been, Hannah glanced around, hoping none of the other church members had noticed her strange reaction. Could they tell who he was just by looking at him?

"Hannah, what's wrong…"

Steffie, who probably preferred "Stephanie" now but hadn't been able to squash the nickname, didn't even get the question out of her mouth before the source of Hannah's problem started up the aisle toward them.

Hannah couldn't answer. Her mouth was dry, and her heart raced. She felt this overwhelming need to run and hide. Why should today be any different? She'd been running and hiding from the truth since the second dot on the home pregnancy test had turned pink.

She stiffened, but she couldn't take her eyes off Todd's steady approach. He looked older than she'd imagined he would, his shoulders even wider than she'd predicted in the well-tailored navy suit he wore. He'd finally filled out his over-six-foot frame and could no longer be called lanky. His hair had deepened to a dark blond, but it still had that tousled look he'd never been able to control.

His face, though, had changed most of all. It was no longer sweet and boyish but was framed with the handsome, hardened planes of manhood. If he'd been smiling, his face probably would have softened and the dimple in his chin would have been more pronounced, but his expression was serious. Cautious.

"Who's he?" Steffie tried again, looking back and forth between the two of them. "Wait. He looks familiar. He looks like…"

The younger woman's words trailed away as Todd reached the front of the room and sidled into the pew behind theirs. Around them, church members continued to make their way toward the exit, but several glanced curiously at Hannah, Todd and Steffie.

"Hi…Hannah." His voice cracked, so he cleared his throat.

He expected her to say something; she knew that. The words just wouldn't come. Words couldn't squeeze past the guilt clawing at her insides. No matter what he'd done, no matter how hurt she'd felt, she should have found a way to tell him as soon as she knew. Or at least she could have found some occasion before Rebecca's fourth birthday. What was she supposed to tell him now?

"Look, I didn't mean to startle you," Todd told her. "I only wanted the chance to—"

"Sweetie, are you okay?" Steffie interrupted, reminding Hannah she was still there, observing entirely too much. "Do you need me to get your dad?"

Hannah shook her head and raised a hand to stop Steffie, but she still couldn't look away from Todd. He appeared just as frozen.

"Is there somewhere we can talk?" he finally choked out. "There are so many things I need to say."

Panic welled deep within her, its acidic tang bitter on her tongue. She couldn't tell him. Not now. Soon, but not yet. She jerked her head, breaking the cold connection of their gazes. Slowly, she started shaking her head and backing toward the aisle.

"I can't do this, Todd. I just can't. I have to go."

Turning, she pressed past Steffie and hurried up the side aisle.

"Hannah! Wait! Stop!"

His plea pounded in her ears, but she couldn't wait. She couldn't stop. She couldn't even look back as she rushed through the vestibule and into the hall leading to the Family Life Center. Rebecca would be waiting for her there in Children's Church.

Hannah could feel his gaze on her as she went, but she didn't hear his footsteps. If he followed her and tried to air out their past right now, he would find out the truth. He would know the secret she'd wasted so much energy trying to keep from him and everyone else. Part of her prayed he would do just that.

Todd watched her go, somehow managing to keep from chasing after her through the church and making a bigger fool of himself than he had already.

She hurried past the line of members shaking hands with the ministry team. Instead of continuing through the glass doors leading to the parking lot, she turned left and headed down a hallway toward the rear of the church.

Only after she'd disappeared completely from sight

did Todd turn his attention to the young woman standing next to him. The tall redhead with a dusting of freckles on her nose was looking at him nearly eye to eye. She raised a delicate brow.

Finally, he remembered his manners and shot out his right hand. "Hi. I'm Todd McBride."

"Todd. Todd." She frowned while rolling the name around on her tongue as if she expected it to ring a bell. Then she shrugged. "I'm Stephanie."

He let go of her hand and then glanced at the sanctuary's rear door again. "I should go after her."

"She didn't seem all that thrilled about talking to you."

"Probably not." He ignored the hopeless feeling threatening to resurface. "But she's going to have to anyway."

With a quick wave, he strode out the door. Finding only Andrew shaking hands and saying goodbye to the last of the stragglers, Todd assumed that Reverend Bob had slipped away to check on his daughter. As inconspicuously as possible, Todd started to follow the same path he'd seen Hannah take.

"Wait, Todd." Andrew caught up to him and gripped his hand in a firm handshake. "Glad you made it. You're probably looking forward to starting your new job. Did the folks at GM Proving Grounds give you a little time to get settled, or did they want you right away?"

"I guess they needed someone right away because I had to negotiate to wait until Tuesday."

"Isn't that just the way it goes? No rest for the weary."

"Guess so." Distracted, Todd cast a furtive glance down the hall. Was she still back there somewhere?

Andrew's gaze followed his. "So, besides Reverend Bob and me, did you see anyone you recognized at the service?"

Todd was barely paying attention, so the words took a moment to sink in. When they did, he turned back to the youth minister. "No disrespect intended, Reverend, but let's not dance around this anymore. We both know I came here to see Hannah."

Andrew nodded, the smile he usually wore absent. "And I noticed that you did see her."

"No one probably knew we were more than friends."

"I knew. Serena knew."

Todd's head came up with a jerk. "Oh."

"Remember that day all of us spent at the beach?"

"I guess so." Of course Todd remembered. It was one of the memories he'd replayed in his mind in the last few years.

"We saw the way you looked at Hannah when you thought no one was watching."

Todd cleared his throat. He could only imagine the emotions that had been written all over his face. Because there didn't seem to be any way to respond to that comment, he changed the subject. "We built a sand castle with Serena's little girl...uh..."

"Tessa," Andrew said to fill in the blank.

"You had a thing for the single mother."

"Still do. But she's married now. To me. Five years." Andrew glanced down at the plain gold band he wore.

"Tessa's got a brother now. Seth. We're having another one in March."

"Wow. Either a lot of time has passed, or you've been busy for a few years," Todd said with a chuckle.

Instead of laughing at his joke, Andrew became serious. "A lot of time has passed."

The words felt like weights being draped across Todd's shoulders. He stared at the floor and waited for whatever else the youth minister had to say.

"Hannah didn't seem happy to see you today."

"I suppose not." Todd reluctantly met the other man's gaze. "I didn't go about things the right way."

"It's hard to know the right thing to do sometimes."

Andrew now wore his concerned minister's face. Todd remembered Hannah once mentioning that Andrew had been a clinical counselor before entering the ministry.

"Apologizing to Hannah is the right thing to do," Todd said. "I know it. She just didn't give me the chance."

"I don't know everything that happened between the two of you or the full reason she ran out of here, but—"

"No," Todd said to interrupt him. "You don't." His sharp tone surprised even him. It wasn't Andrew's fault that Hannah had refused to talk to him. He had no one to blame for that but himself. Taking a deep breath to clear his thoughts, he tried again. "I've been waiting five years to talk to Hannah…about a lot of things."

"Have you ever considered that healing this relationship might not be as easy as you've imagined?"

"You mean that it might be too late? Sure, I've thought about it." *A lot.* He took a long breath and shook his head in frustration. "But I have to do the right thing. I've prayed about it, and I'm convinced it's what God wants me to do, so I'm just going to have to find a way to get Hannah to listen to me."

"You sound pretty determined."

"I am."

"I guess you'll be needing this then."

Andrew withdrew a pen and notebook from his pocket, wrote something on it and handed to him. It said, "Hannah," and it had a street address and an apartment number on it. Todd drew his eyebrows together as he looked up from it.

"You didn't think she still lived at home, did you?"

He answered with a shrug. As a matter of fact, he had. He'd already driven by his old home and that particular house next door several times since he'd arrived in town on Friday. He'd studied that familiar dwelling, wondering whether she was inside and hoping she would pick that moment to go out to her car.

Todd closed his hand over the slip of paper. "Thanks, Andrew."

"Will you do me one favor when you talk to Hannah?" Andrew waited for his nod before he continued, "When you're talking, will you be sure to listen, too?"

Of course he would listen, Todd thought as he climbed in his car and turned out of the church lot onto Hickory Ridge Road. He would listen, but he couldn't imagine what Hannah would have to say. She had nothing to apologize for; that was his department alone. Yet, an uncomfortable sensation settled between his shoulder blades. Why did he get the sense that Andrew knew something he didn't?

"What are you doing, Mommy?"

Hannah turned from the medicine cabinet mirror where she was repairing her makeup. Rebecca, dressed only in a pair of red cotton tights, underwear and a lace-trimmed undershirt, stared up at her from the bathroom doorway.

Quickly, Hannah turned her back to her daughter and brushed the last of her tears away with the back of her hand. "Nothing, honey. You go ahead and finish changing your clothes. Remember to lay your dress out on the bed so I can hang it up, okay?"

"Okay," Rebecca answered, though she would likely forget and leave the Christmas plaid dress in a pile on the floor. She started to leave and then stopped, turning back to her mother. "Are you crying?"

"No. Not really." Hannah pressed her lips together. Now she was even lying to her daughter. When would it all stop? "I guess I am a little sad."

"Don't be sad, Mommy." Rebecca wrapped her arms around her mother's thighs and squeezed.

"Go on now," she said, fighting back another wave of emotion.

As soon as Rebecca skipped down the hall, Hannah started swiping at the dampness again. She'd managed to hold herself together all through the ritual of collecting her daughter from her church program and through the drive home, but Hannah's control had wavered the moment she was alone, changing out of her church clothes.

Todd? In Milford again? Come to think of it, she didn't even know why he was in town. She might know that answer now if she'd given him a chance to speak. But how could she? Without any notice, she wasn't prepared to face him. Who was she kidding? Even with six months' notice, she wouldn't have been able to come up with a valid explanation for what she'd done.

All of her excuses for not telling him—her anger for his leaving, her choice to never reveal the identity of her child's father, her rationalization that Todd didn't deserve to know—now sounded like the incoherent ramblings of a teenage girl.

That was what they were.

How could she ever have thought she had the right to withhold the information from him that he was a father? No one had that right to wield so much power over other people's lives.

She had to tell him; that was a given. And she would. Soon. She just needed a little time to regroup first. After that, she would ask around and find out whom he was visiting and how long he would stay. She would tell him everything then, but she would do it on her terms.

Hannah nodded at the mirror, her thoughts clear for the first time since Todd appeared at her church and tilted her world on its axis.

A knock at the front door, though, set her thoughts

and her newly settled world spinning once again. Was it Todd already? No, it couldn't be. He wouldn't even know where she lived, although he would only have to ask her father to get that information. Reverend Bob, who still didn't know the whole truth, either.

Rebecca reappeared in the bathroom, this time wearing a reindeer sweatshirt with her tights. "Somebody's knocking on the door."

"I heard. I'll get the door. Why don't you go put your jeans on? Then go set up your dolls in the living room, and I'll be there in a minute to play."

Again, Rebecca scurried off, but this time, Hannah followed, turning down the hall to the front door. She stopped as her hand touched the wood. Without a peephole to check for sure, she could only hold her breath and hope she was wrong.

Lord, please don't let it be Todd. It's too soon. Please give me strength when the time comes. Amen.

Her hand was on the doorknob when his voice came through the door.

"Hannah, it's me. Todd. I know you're in there. I can see the lights."

Panic came in a rush that clenched inside her and dampened her palms. No. She couldn't tell him now. She wasn't ready. Not yet.

"Go away, Todd."

Though she recognized the voice as her own, the words surprised even her. She was taking the easy way out again rather than facing this mess she'd created, but she couldn't seem to help herself.

For a few seconds, there was no sound on the other side of the door. She almost expected to hear the crunch of snow as he trudged down the steps and away from her apartment, but instead there was a more insistent knock.

"You might as well open the door because I'm not leaving."

Hannah stared at the door. Todd sounded different. The laid-back boy she remembered had been replaced by this determined and forceful guy she didn't recognize at all, and yet she still found herself cracking the door open to him. *Whatever happened to your fear of strangers?* But irony encased that thought, for even this new Todd was in no way a stranger to her.

He stood on the porch, the collar of his wool jacket flipped up to shield his ears and his hands shoved in the front pockets of his slacks. Several years on an island off the southern end of the Malay Peninsula hadn't prepared him for a Milford December. She was surprised by the impulse to warm his hands with her own, but she remained behind the cracked door.

"How did you find out where I live?"

"Andrew gave me your address." He withdrew his hand from his pocket and held out a crumpled piece of paper.

"Why did Andrew—" she started to ask but stopped herself when the answer dawned.

Have you told Todd? Andrew's words from that long-ago night flashed through her mind. The youth minister and his future wife, Serena, had counseled her when she'd first discovered she was pregnant. She'd denied

Andrew's assertion that Todd was the father, and neither of them had pressured her to reveal her secret.

The secret that had come back to haunt her today.

Hannah sighed, suddenly exhausted by the energy it had required to keep the truth hidden. "Todd, what are you doing here?"

Todd's teeth chattered as he zipped his jacket higher. "I told you I want to talk to you."

She cocked her head to the side and studied him. Now that the shock of seeing him was beginning to wear off, old, mixed emotions began to resurface. Anger she realized she had no right to feel and long-buried hurt collided, leaving her insides feeling exposed. "After five years? Why would we have anything to talk about?"

"We do. I know *I* do."

Hannah stared at him. He'd surprised her again with his certainty when she felt so unsure. "Maybe in a few days but not yet. I'm not ready—"

As she spoke those last three words, she started closing the door. Todd pressed his foot into the space before it could close completely.

"Isn't five years long enough?" he said.

Staring at his dress shoe, Hannah waited, but he didn't say more, so she finally lifted her gaze to his. In his eyes was a look of anguish so stark that Hannah could only remember seeing an expression like it once before. She'd found it in the mirror the day that Todd's family left for the airport.

He glanced away and back, and the look was gone.

"I've waited five years to apologize to you. I'm not leaving until you let me do it."

Hannah blinked, her mind racing. A million times she'd imagined Todd's reaction when she told him the truth. Now she only wanted to run and hide with her secret again, to protect her daughter from the fallout and herself from the blame she deserved.

But she couldn't run anymore. Todd was right. It was time.

"Then I guess I'd better invite you in."

Chapter Three

As Hannah pulled open the door, Todd released the breath he hadn't even realized he'd been holding. His foot ached, more likely from standing out in the cold than from where she'd squeezed it in the door, but he didn't care. He was here, she was here, and that was all that mattered.

"Nice place," he said before he even stepped on the mat and took a look around.

And it was nice. Though one of the four smallish apartments in a renovated older house, Hannah had made it look warm and homey with overstuffed furniture and soft pillows. It was decorated in earth tones and dotted with artistic, framed black-and-white photographs of children.

The Christmas tree he'd first glimpsed through the front window radiated warmth, as well, with its homemade ornaments, popcorn strands and spatter of silvery icicles. No hand-blown glass balls and fussy velvet bows for Hannah's apartment.

The woman herself looked as warm and casual as her house, dressed in well-worn jeans and a black long-sleeved top. She had fuzzy slippers on her feet. But her expression showed she was anything but comfortable with him in her space, and she looked as if she'd been crying.

"Yes, we like it."

We? The smile that had formed on his face slipped away as he turned to her. What had he missed? Hannah took a few steps into the living room and motioned for Todd to follow.

There in the corner that he couldn't see from the front door was a tiny blond girl, surrounded by baby dolls, blankets and play bottles. For several seconds, Todd stared at the child who was looking back at him with huge, haunting eyes. She looked familiar somehow.

"Come here, honey," Hannah called to the child. When the little girl stood under her protective arm, Hannah turned back to face him.

"Todd, this is Rebecca. She's my daughter."

Daughter? Hannah had a daughter? He looked back and forth between them, his thoughts spinning. Though their features were slightly different, they both had lovely peachy skin and light, light hair. They were clearly relatives.

When he glanced away to collect his thoughts, his gaze landed again on the amazing photos dotting the walls on either side of the Christmas tree. The subjects of those photos, taken in a variety of natural backdrops, weren't children, but rather one child—the same sweet-looking little girl standing right in front of him.

Clearing his throat, he turned back to them. "Nice pictures."

"Thanks."

"The photographer did a great job."

She nodded but didn't look at the portraits. Instead, she turned to her daughter. "Rebecca, this is Mr. McBride."

"Hi," she said quickly before taking refuge behind her mother's jeans-clad leg.

"Hello, Rebecca."

Todd shook his head, trying to reconcile the new information. Parts of this puzzle weren't fitting together easily. Was Hannah married now? Was that what Andrew had been trying to tell him when he'd suggested that healing the relationship might not be easy? If that was it, how could the minister have been so cruel as to let him go on believing…hoping?

His gaze fell to Hannah's left hand, the one she was using to lead the child back to her toys and out of earshot of their conversation.

Hannah wore no ring.

Suddenly all of Todd's other questions fell away as one pressed to the forefront of his mind: a question too personal for him to ask. Still, when she returned to him, he took hold of her arm and led her around the corner to the entry so he could ask it.

"Who's her father, Hannah?"

She shot a glance back at her daughter, as if she worried Rebecca had overheard. He couldn't blame her if she shouted, "How dare you" for the private question and more. He deserved it.

But instead of yelling, she began in a soft tone. "You have to understand—"

"Who is it?" He couldn't help it. He didn't want an explanation; he wanted a name. Jealousy he had no right to feel swelled inside him, burning and destroying. The thought of another man touching her left his heart raw. If only he and Hannah had waited, their story might have turned out differently. Hannah might have been his wife. Her child, theirs.

Hannah stared back at him incredulously, as if she was shocked that he'd had the gall to ask. It wasn't about wanting; he *had* to know.

"Is it that blond guy from church?"

"Grant?" Her eyes widened and then she shook her head. "He's just a friend."

"Do I know him then?"

"Of course you do." She spat the words.

Strange, she sounded exasperated. She seemed to think he was an idiot for not knowing the answer. He stepped around the corner and studied the child again. She was so fair and beautiful, just like her mother. Rebecca must have sensed his attention on her because she looked up from her dolls and smiled at him.

And he knew.

His gut clenched, and he felt helpless to do anything but stare. Why it wasn't immediately apparent to him he couldn't imagine now. Her green eyes had looked familiar because he saw eyes like those in the mirror every morning.

Though he was no expert on children's ages and this particular child was probably small for her age, as her mother had been, he could see from her features that she wasn't a toddler. Rebecca looked about four years old, just old enough to have been conceived five years before.

"She's mine, isn't she?"

Hannah didn't answer, but her eyes filled and a few tears escaped to trail down her cheeks. She brushed them away with the backs of her hands.

"Tell me I'm right, Hannah. Am I Rebecca's father?"

Instead of nodding the way he was certain she would, Hannah shook her head. Her jaw flexed as if she was gritting her teeth.

"How could you have thought—" She stopped whatever she'd been about to say. Closing her eyes, she pressed her hands over her closed lids and took a few deep breaths before continuing. "If you're asking if you supplied half of her DNA, then you're right. But for her whole life, I've been both parents to Rebecca. She's mine. Just mine."

"Not just yours. She's mine, too."

Todd wasn't sure whether he'd spoken those words aloud or just in the privacy of his heart until Hannah stalked from the room and crouched down by her daughter. *No, their daughter.*

Maybe he hadn't said the right thing, but what did

she expect when she'd just dropped a bomb like that? He didn't know what to *think,* let alone what to say.

How naive he'd been with his big plans to return here and to earn Hannah's forgiveness and her heart. He'd thought he and Hannah were the only two involved, that their old conflicts were only between the two of them, when a third person had been growing inside Hannah before he'd ever left.

Father. He couldn't wrap his thoughts around the title yet, let alone apply it to himself. Everything he knew about himself changed with that single admission.

"Why did you have to come back?" Hannah whispered when she returned to him, appearing more agitated than before. "We were doing fine. Just fine. Now you've messed all of that up. We'll never be the same."

"Come on, Hannah. We have a lot to talk about."

"I don't think so. You've got your answer now, so go."

"I can't leave now that you've told me this."

"Please go." Her eyes filled again.

Her plea tore at his heart. Clearly, they had more to say to each other, but maybe now wasn't the best time. He was still too shocked, too confused to make any decisions that would affect their lives. Three lives.

"I won't stay gone, you know. I'm living in Milford now, and I'm sticking around this time."

Either she didn't hear him or she refused to answer, but Hannah hurried him toward the door and closed it behind him. As the cold enfolded him, this time seeping to his very core rather than only touching his extremities, Todd realized that Hannah was right about one thing: None of them would ever be the same.

It wasn't until Todd was back at his Commerce Road town house and eating chicken noodle soup that refused to warm his chilled insides that he realized he'd never apologized to Hannah. After traveling from the other side of the world in miles and in years of effort, he hadn't even managed to do the most important thing he'd come to town to accomplish.

"You were too busy trying not to swallow your tongue to remember anything else," he said to the stacked boxes around him.

Sitting at the new glass dinette in the kitchen, he stared down into the soup bowl and stirred the noodles into a whirlpool. His thoughts traveled in a similar circular pattern, but unlike the liquid, they wouldn't stop spinning.

A child. His child. Of course, he should have considered the possibility that Hannah could have become pregnant. He knew the textbook mechanics of reproduction and the potential consequences of unprotected sex, but he'd never once considered that they might have made a child together. He and Hannah had only made love that one time. Apparently, it only took once.

The returned letters and unanswered calls made sense now. Not only had he left her alone with her guilt over what had happened between them, but he'd also left her alone with his child.

Alone. He felt that way now as he sat with only the

bare walls and the truth to keep him company. He suddenly felt a stronger need to connect with his parents than he had at any time since he'd hugged them goodbye in Kranji a week earlier. But what would he say to them if he called? He could just imagine how that conversation would go: "Hello, Mom and Dad. Or should I say Grandma and Grandpa? I have just the best news."

He shook his head. No, that conversation would have to wait for another day when he was prepared to hear disappointment of that magnitude over international phone lines. He wasn't ready for that when he hadn't digested it himself yet.

But there was one call he could make now. He pulled out the phone book, looked up the name and dialed. He didn't even identify himself when the man answered on the second ring.

"Why didn't you tell me?" Todd said simply.

Andrew Westin sighed loudly into the line. "Todd. I had an idea I would be hearing from you."

"You could have saved yourself the call by telling me before."

"You make it sound so easy."

His jaw was so tightly clenched in frustration that it took Todd a few seconds to be able to answer at all and a few seconds more to answer civilly. "It was easy. The first time I called the church, you could have said, 'Hey, Todd, it's good to hear from you. Just thought you should know, you're a dad.'"

"Sure, I could have done that."

"Then why didn't you?"

"It wasn't my place. Then or now."

Todd stalked over to the tan striped couch, dropped onto it and sank into the backrest. "Then or now? What do you mean by that?"

"Hannah never told anyone who the father of her baby was. Until now."

"Until now?" Todd straightened in his seat. There could be no slouching after a comment like that, one that crushed as much as it confused. Hannah had been more ashamed of him than she'd been of being an unwed mother. He didn't know what to do with that information.

"Wait. Then how did *you* know?"

"I told you Serena and I had guessed you two were more than friends when we saw you together."

Todd swallowed. "Oh."

"So, when Hannah became pregnant, we suspected. Then when little Rebecca arrived, we…well, knew."

The image of those pretty green eyes filled his mind again. If Andrew and Serena had already been suspecting, he could easily see how they'd connected the dots to solve the puzzle. They'd probably put it together faster than he had.

"What about Reverend Bob?"

"If he knows, he's never mentioned it to me." Andrew paused. "Bob was always more concerned with supporting his daughter than tracking down his grandchild's father."

"Another reason I never found out the truth."

"Todd, I always thought she would open up eventually, that *she* would tell you. But she didn't. So when you called looking for answers, I figured God was suggesting that I help the truth along."

"I don't know whether to say thanks or not." Todd shoved his free hand through his hair.

"But you know now, right?"

Todd blew out a breath. "Yes, I know."

"And how do you feel about that?"

"Don't use all that psychobabble on me, okay, Reverend?"

"Fine. But she's a cute one, your daughter."

Emotion filled Todd's throat with a speed that surprised him. Rebecca was his daughter, and she didn't even know him.

"Yeah…she's beautiful," he choked out finally.

Andrew chuckled into the line. "Spoken like a true father. I do have one more question for you."

"What's that?"

"What are you going to do about it now that you know?"

What are you going to do? Todd didn't have an answer for the minister's question or for his own as they said their goodbyes. He clicked off the phone and laid it on the end table. It was a given that he would take some responsibility for the care of his child. His parents would expect that, and he expected that of himself. He didn't even want to remember all the other things he'd expected to happen when he returned to Milford.

Disquiet had him pushing off the sofa and crossing to the light wood bookshelf he'd just purchased and already had crammed with books. His fingers closed over a heavy cloth-covered album his mother had insisted he take with him on the plane at Changi International Airport. He took it back to the table and plunked it next to the bowl of soup that had already congealed.

He sat and opened it to the first page. It was as he predicted: a tribute to the lives and loves of the Mc-Bride clan. He would expect nothing less from Sharon McBride than a maudlin display, sure to cause more homesickness than to cure it.

The first few pages were all family pictures, both of the posed professional variety and informal shots taken in front of their homes in Milford and then in Kranji. His mother had a talent for pulling heartstrings.

Todd flipped through images of himself eating his first birthday cake, standing proudly on the first day of kindergarten and marching in the high school band. Then came photos of his friends in Singapore and even a few of Todd and Hannah hanging out at the Milford Memories festival. Because those last shots tempted him to feel sorry for himself, he turned the page.

The next pictures made him smile: first the wedding portrait of Roy McBride and the former Sharon Quinn and then a few other black-and-white snapshots of the two of them as children.

When Todd reached the last yellowing image at the bottom right, he stopped. He stared at the little girl looking out at him from the paper. In the white trim at the photo's bottom edge, someone had written in a slanted script, "Sharon, age four," but the picture could just as easily have been of Hannah's child. Not subtle like the similarity his daughter had to him, the resemblance between his mother and Rebecca was so obvious that at the same age they could have been twins.

Why that was the trigger—this mirror image—Todd couldn't explain, and yet he was suddenly furious. His hands clasped the edge of the table so hard he could feel the glass side imprinting on his palm. His jaw flexed, and he could feel his pulse beating at his temple.

How could Hannah not have told him? No matter what he'd done, no matter how angry she was with him or how much she wanted to cast him as the villain who deserved all the blame, he still had the right to know he'd fathered a child. The chance to *be* a father to his child.

He'd deserved the truth.

Would he have been a great father at seventeen? It was hard to say, but he'd deserved the chance to try. So much time had already passed. Rebecca was four years old. Whether she'd done it consciously or not, Hannah had stolen that time from them, time they could never get back.

The whole situation just didn't make sense. The Hannah he'd known could never have been so cruel as to keep this monumental secret from him. Then a thought struck him at his foundation. Maybe he hadn't known her at all. Maybe the girl he'd fallen in love with had only existed in his mind, and the future he'd planned for them was just as much of an illusion.

None of what he thought before could matter. Everything was different now that he knew about Rebecca. He still wanted to apologize to Hannah for past events, but the present was much more important. They needed to discuss Rebecca's care and to work out a plan for him to get to know his daughter.

Hannah would fight him on that, he was sure, but she didn't know him, either, if she thought that battle would be an easy one. Maybe he hadn't fought hard enough when Hannah had decided to eliminate him from her life five years ago, but he'd done a lot of growing up since then—physically and spiritually. Hannah had just better get it through her mind that he was here and he wasn't going away.

Chapter Four

"I'm hungry," Rebecca announced as she raced through the front door her mother had just unlocked. "When are we going to eat dinner?"

Hannah somehow managed to keep her sigh a silent one as she followed behind her with several plastic grocery bags draped over each arm. It wasn't Rebecca's fault that Hannah's day had been lousy, or even that they'd had to stop at the grocery store on the way home from Mrs. Nelson's because there wasn't any food in the house.

Hannah had no one to blame for either of those things but herself. When Todd had finally left Sunday, she'd been too exhausted to even think about grocery shopping for the week. She'd barely been able to just keep her promise and play dolls with Rebecca.

As they'd sat together on the floor, diapering, swaddling and feeding two hairless baby dolls with plastic milk and juice bottles, her thoughts kept returning to another baby and the father who'd just been blindsided by her existence. Would Hannah ever be able to forget the look of bewilderment that had strained his features? Even the fresh ache she felt every time she remembered that Todd hadn't immediately recognized Rebecca as his child couldn't compete with that. Still, it hurt her that he'd assumed she'd been intimate with someone other than him.

I won't stay gone. As they had several times in the twenty-four hours since he'd spoken them, his words echoed in her thoughts. Until the evening service and after it, she'd sat anxious and alert, waiting for him to make good on his promise.

All she'd gotten for her trouble was a sleepless night and a drowsy day at work when she needed to be sharp while doing year-end accounting for several small businesses. Too many more days like that and she could add joblessness to her list of problems.

"Mommy, didn't you hear me? I'm hungry." This time Rebecca said it in the woeful tone of the starving. She still hadn't learned that mothers often heard even when they didn't answer.

"Have patience, sweetie. Your chicken nuggets are coming right up."

At least they would come up as soon as Hannah preheated the oven and baked them for twenty to twenty-five minutes, but she didn't want to give Rebecca that bad news and risk a meltdown. That was the last thing she needed when her friend, Grant Sumner, would arrive at any time for the home-cooked meal Hannah had promised him weeks ago. She didn't even have the pork chops defrosted.

A bachelor who claimed an allergy to anything domestic, Grant already could recite every take-out menu in Milford verbatim. He didn't need her ordering a pizza on the one night when he could have been enjoying home cooking.

"But I'm hungry now," Rebecca whined. "Can I have a cookie?"

Irritation welled in her, but Hannah forced it back. "Maybe after dinner."

Already, Rebecca was cuing up the waterworks, so Hannah grabbed the first distraction that came to mind. "Why don't you watch your video until dinner's ready?"

"Yay, TV!"

Her daughter's glee came with its own sting of reproach. Hannah was convinced she was a bad mother now. She'd even started using "Aunt TV" as a nanny. "Just for a few minutes. Mr. Grant should be here soon for dinner."

Rebecca hurried off before the offer of the rare visual treat evaporated with the arrival of company.

As if he recognized his cue, Grant rang the bell, pushed the unlocked door wide and stepped inside.

"Hannah, you know better than to leave your door unlocked like that. Anyone can walk right in off the street and—"

"Yeah, yeah, I know," Hannah interrupted, smirking at her friend over the fact that he'd done just that.

Grant flushed in a way his fair skin failed to hide

and shrugged out of his coat, hanging it on the coat tree next to the door. "You know what I mean."

"Of course I do. And thanks for worrying about me."

"Somebody's got to do it." As Grant started pushing the door closed, another pair of hands on the other side stopped it.

"Hannah, it's me." Todd's voice slipped through the crack.

"Me?" Grant yanked the door back open and came face-to-face with the man a few years younger and a couple of inches taller. "Who are you?"

"Todd McBride." With that curt answer, Todd pressed past him into the entry. "Who's asking?"

"Grant Sumner, Hannah's—"

"Friend," she finished before Grant had the chance.

Hannah didn't miss the confusion in Grant's eyes or the irritation in Todd's, but she wasn't about to have a scene here with Rebecca in the next room. "Todd, this really isn't a good time."

Grant shot her a perplexed glance but jumped in with his support. "Yeah, sorry, buddy. We were just getting ready to have dinner."

Todd's jaw tightened, but he stood where he was. "It's never going to be a good time to—"

Hannah put her hand up to cut him off before he could say more. "I wish you would have called first."

"You mean so that you could *not* answer." Todd closed the door behind him and stood in front of it with his arms crossed. "Been there, done that. I'm over it. How about you?" His gaze locked with hers and wouldn't let go.

"What are you two talking about?"

At Grant's words, Hannah could finally pull her gaze away. Her friend was staring at them both by turns, and then he faced her alone.

"It's him, isn't it? He's the reason—"

Grant managed to stop himself before he said more, but Hannah ached for his hurt feelings. That she'd never led him to believe there could be more than friendship between them didn't seem to exonerate her for putting him in this awkward situation.

"I'm sorry, Grant," she found herself saying, though she couldn't imagine what she would say next.

Rather that looking at her for confirmation of his assumption, Grant turned back to Todd. "Maybe you'd just better leave right now."

Todd started out by holding his hands wide. "Look, friend, I don't have a problem with you, but—"

"I'm not your friend." Grant took a step toward Todd, but instead of holding his hands wide, he had them tight by his sides, fisted. "But I am Hannah's. And since she doesn't seem to want you here…"

Immediately, Todd's posture tightened, and he stepped forward, as well. "Don't you think that's her decision?"

"She already said this isn't a good time."

Hannah couldn't believe her eyes as she looked back and forth between them. With all this male posturing, they looked like a pair of gorillas, pounding their chests and announcing their dominance. The two of them standing their ground, just feet apart, would have been comical if the situation hadn't been so *not* funny. Her daughter was right in the next room.

Stepping to the side, Hannah peered into the living room. Rebecca was sprawled on the floor in front of the TV with her elbows jutting out and her head cradled between her tiny hands. Maybe "Aunt TV" wasn't so bad just this once.

When she returned to the front hall, Hannah stepped between the two men. "You know, maybe we should all just call it a night. Can I give you a rain check on dinner, Grant? I didn't get started the way I'd planned, anyway."

Grant gave her a distracted glance. "That's fine, Hannah. I'll just show him the door first." He pointed around her at Todd.

"I'm not leaving again until Hannah and I have some things settled, so you can go ahead."

Sidestepping Hannah, Grant faced Todd again. "Can't you see she doesn't want you here?"

"And can't you see this is between Hannah and me? I'm her friend, too—at least I was, once upon a time."

"Some kind of friend you were." Grant spat the words. "Friends don't take advantage of an innocent girl and leave her alone and pregnant."

"Stop it, you two!" Hannah looked around when she realized she'd raised her voice, but since Rebecca didn't scurry into the room, she figured she hadn't been as loud as she thought. Still, she spoke at just above a whisper. "I mean it."

Todd looked directly at Grant, not appearing to have heard Hannah at all. "It wasn't like that. I lo—" He stopped himself, waving his hand as if to wipe away what he'd almost said.

That nearly spoken word stopped Hannah when she should have been shoving both Neanderthals toward the door. After everything, Todd still claimed he'd loved her back then. Maybe he really remembered it that way, though it had probably just been infatuation, just a teen-age hormone-induced haze. She knew that feeling well. She'd made the same mistaken assumption in her own heart.

"You don't know anything about it," Todd said to Grant.

"I've been around for the last few years. That's more than you can say."

Todd tilted his chin up. "I'm here now."

"For how long?"

Grant posed the question, but Hannah was dying to know the answer to it.

"Not that it's any of your business, but I start a job at GM Proving Grounds tomorrow. I'm here in town. To stay."

"What if she doesn't want you here? What if *no one* wants you here?"

Todd raised his hands in surrender. "Resent me all you want. It doesn't change the fact that I'm Rebecca's father, and I intend to have some kind of relationship with her no matter what you think."

Hannah gasped and closed her eyes. *Please God.*

Please God. Tell me she didn't hear. But when she opened her eyes again, the expressions on both men's faces told her the bad news before she could even turn toward the living room. In the doorway, Rebecca stared at Todd, her eyes wide with amazement. Finally, she turned back to Hannah.

"Is it true, Mommy? Is Mr. McBride my dad?"

Todd let the phone ring four times, waiting for the answering machine to pick up as it had each time he'd called Monday night and again since he'd been home from work that day. This time the machine didn't answer, which could only mean that Hannah had returned from work and had shut it off.

Too bad he couldn't turn off his guilt over last evening's events as easily as she'd switched off the power. If he continued to be as distracted at work as he'd been on his first day at the Proving Grounds, then he wouldn't have to worry about having a job for too long.

With the phone continuing to ring, Todd switched the handset from one ear to the other, as he shed his maroon-and-white pin-striped dress shirt. He was already sitting on the edge of the bed in his undershirt and trousers when something clicked on the other end of the line.

"Hello," a small voice said.

His breath caught, but he forced words anyway. "Hi, Rebecca. This is your— This is Mr. McBride."

"Hi," she said automatically. Then she added an uncomfortable "oh."

He frowned. After Hannah had insisted that both he and Grant leave, she had probably initiated a heart-to-heart talk with their daughter. What a four-year-old would be able to understand from this impossible mess, he hadn't a clue. He barely understood parts of it himself. Whatever else Hannah had told his daughter, he guessed from Rebecca's surprised reaction that her mother had also said they wouldn't be seeing him anymore.

That's where she was wrong. He hadn't just found out he was a father and then faced his parents' extreme disappointment when he'd told them they were grandparents, only to be shut out of his daughter's life.

He was still coming up with something to say to Rebecca when he heard another voice in the background.

"Sweetie, do you remember that I told you not to answer the phone?" Hannah said.

"But it's…Mr. McBride."

After some muffled voices and footsteps, Hannah's voice came on the line. "Would you please stop calling here? I had to unplug the machine."

"I'm sorry about yesterday."

"You and Grant—what you did was unforgivable. This time you hurt my child."

"*Our* child," he corrected, though he couldn't argue with the rest of what Hannah had said. "I didn't want Rebecca to find out that way any more than you did."

"So why'd you tell her?"

"You were there. You know I didn't intentionally—"

"Anyone who knows the first thing about parenting knows that children hear and see everything that's going on around them."

"Whose fault is it I don't know—" He managed to stop his retort before he said, "How to be Rebecca's father." Hannah was at fault for that, but as far as he could tell, there was plenty of blame to go around. He wasn't going to make any progress by pelting her with accusations.

After counting from ten backward, he tried again. "Okay, this isn't about fault, but she knows now. We have to deal with that…together."

"I've already dealt with that." Her voice screeched at the end of her sentence. "Just like I've dealt with everything else in her life. Neither of us needs you or your help."

"Hannah, I might have let you do it before, but I'm not going to allow you to cut me out this time."

"Me cut *you* out?" She became quiet for a few seconds, as if she realized she'd said more than she intended. Finally, she sighed. "Don't you think you've done enough?"

"No! I haven't done enough."

What happened to that patience he'd just found? But the fact remained: He hadn't done anything to care for Hannah or to provide for their daughter's needs. That he hadn't been given the chance didn't change the bottom line.

"Don't call anymore, Todd. I won't answer."

The connection went dead as she clicked off the phone. He didn't bother dialing again. She would probably just leave it off the hook, anyway, and even if she didn't, she would be screening his calls.

Todd ignored the hopelessness threatening to take hold in his heart. He couldn't give up, not when there was so much at stake—more now than even a teen romance that had seemed so real at the time. This was about their daughter, and Rebecca deserved to have a father in her life.

A week before, Todd never would have imagined himself admitting this, but he wasn't sure he even wanted a future with Hannah. At least not this Hannah. She was cold and selfish and spiteful. *Is she also hurt and scared?* Todd wanted to ignore that charitable thought. He didn't want to forgive her yet, and that appeared to be just what his heart was tempted to do.

"Lord, why do I have to be the one to keep taking the first step?" he whispered.

But the answer was so clear in his thoughts it was as if God Himself had spoken the words. *Because she can't.* For whatever reason, Hannah couldn't be the one to offer an olive branch. Though his hurt was new, his wounds fresh, Hannah had been harboring hers for a lot longer, allowing them to fester instead of heal. Forgiveness was never easy, but he guessed that it became harder to give over time.

Still, he couldn't allow Hannah's problem with forgiveness to keep him from knowing his daughter. Every day that passed with Hannah nursing her resentment was another day he and Rebecca couldn't be together.

That was as unacceptable as Hannah avoiding him by refusing to take his calls.

Suddenly, an idea began forming in his thoughts. Once before, Hannah had been able to avoid him when she'd wanted to, but this time there were no parents, oceans or continents separating them. Just a few traffic lights, the Huron River and a tiny, downtown shopping district.

Since the choices of destinations were limited in Milford, even outside church and school, friends crossed paths whenever they bought a quart of milk at Breen's IGA, picked out end tables at Huron Valley Furniture or even grabbed a Coney dog or some Thai food from one of those new joints on North Main.

If seeing friends and neighbors regularly was so easy, he imagined that the opposite was true, as well: Avoiding someone a person didn't want to see would be almost impossible. Because Hannah was on a tight budget, she probably wasn't in the market often for new end tables, but she needed milk frequently, and she probably craved a good Coney once in a while.

Todd finally understood John Mellencamp's 1980s anthem, celebrating life in a "Small Town." Milford was a small town, all right. Hannah was about to find out just how small.

Chapter Five

Hannah had tried her best to make it as normal a Sunday morning as possible. She'd hurried Rebecca through their morning routine, and she'd actively contributed to the discussion in her young adult Sunday school class. Even now she was chatting with several women in the vestibule as she usually did, but nothing about this morning or the last few days had felt normal—not with Todd appearing like a case of indigestion everywhere she went.

The conversation continued around her, but Hannah couldn't help but divide her attention between it and the door where Andrew Westin greeted members and guests. She expected one of them to be Todd, and she couldn't decide whether she would be more disappointed if he showed up or if he didn't.

"Hannah, are you with us?"

She turned back to catch Julia Sims grinning at her, excitement dancing in her dark, heavily lashed eyes.

"You're missing the news."

"What news is that?"

Charity McKinley, Julia's half sister, who was the golden opposite to her raven-dark looks, wore the expression of the cat who had swallowed the canary. Charity reached out her hands to Steffie Wilmington and Serena Jacobs, encouraging those two and several others into a tight circle.

"It's finally happened. I'm pregnant," she said in the quietest voice possible for someone fairly bursting with excitement.

"Congratulations," Hannah said, stepping forward to hug Charity. She was thrilled that God had blessed her friend, who'd longed for a child since she and Rick had married four years before.

"That's wonderful," Serena agreed. "Rick must be thrilled."

Though it seemed impossible, Charity's smile widened. "That and he's turned into this broccoli-and-whole-grains-toting drill sergeant. 'Here, sweetheart, eat wheat germ. It's for the baby.'" She imitated her husband's deep voice but she finished with a laugh.

"Was your mom thrilled with the news?" Hannah asked her.

"She's already knitting booties."

"I'm happy for her, too." It was great to see healing in Charity's relationship with her mother, Laura Sims, after their painful rift from a few years before. But rather than dampen Charity's excitement by mentioning difficult memories, Hannah changed the subject.

"Looks like our church is having a population explosion."

"Look what you started," Julia said, shaking an index finger at Serena, whose swollen belly announced her new arrival, expected in March.

Serena rested her hands on her stomach. "I love being a trendsetter."

"I don't know about the rest of you," Steffie said, pausing for effect before she added, "but if I was newlywed, I wouldn't be drinking the water here."

Immediately the other women turned to Tricia Williams Lancaster. Married just over a year to Michigan State Police Trooper Brett Lancaster, Tricia definitely still qualified as a newlywed, though she already had three children with her late first husband, Rusty.

"I'll be sure to keep that in mind," Tricia said.

Tricia turned her head as if in search of a new topic, and her face brightened as a square-jawed man with a military haircut and a football player's shoulders squeezed through the doorway.

"If that's not Trooper Joe Rossetti in the flesh and in a *church* on a Sunday morning," Tricia said with a grin. "God does work in mysterious ways."

"Brett's friend?" Julia craned her neck for a better look at the handsome State Police trooper. "I thought you said Brett had been inviting him for months. How'd he get him here? Tell him there was an illegal arms sale in the church basement?"

"No, even better. We promised to stuff him with

Sunday dinner after church. What starving single guy can resist that?"

They were all having a laugh over that when Serena suddenly stopped. "Uh, Hannah…"

The youth minister's wife was staring at the entry where her husband had kept his post, and Hannah didn't have to stretch her imagination to guess who'd just come through the door. She spun around in time to see Todd shaking hands with Andrew, but he barely glanced at her before opening the side door and entering the sanctuary.

"It's the guy from last Sunday," Steffie exclaimed. "What's the story—" she began again, but one of the others cleared her throat to interrupt her.

Slowly, Hannah faced her friends, bracing herself for their questions. Though they couldn't conceal the curiosity in their expressions, no one spoke up, and the one who might have asked was discouraged by Charity's staying hand on her shoulder.

They knew about Todd—at least they had to suspect by now. Serena knew far more than the others, and Andrew had probably discussed Todd's arrival with her, as well. Of the others who hadn't witnessed the scene in the sanctuary last Sunday, they surely had heard about it. Unfortunately, scandalous information sometimes traveled faster than the *Good News,* even in churches.

Still, her friends didn't ask. She should have expected as much. God had blessed her with true friends. They wouldn't pressure her. They would simply wait until she was ready to tell them.

The first notes of the organ prelude saved her from having to decide whether or not she was ready today. Certain rules of etiquette applied to the preacher's daughter, and one of them made it a no-no for her to race into services late.

"I'd better get in there," she said, clasping her Bible tightly under her arm to keep from fidgeting.

"I'll go with you," Steffie said. "Where's Grant this morning?"

Hannah stiffened as she pulled open the sanctuary door. "I'm not sure."

Some amazing friend she was. Hannah hadn't even noticed that Grant was absent, even though Steffie and she usually sat with him during Sunday-morning services. She hoped he wasn't staying away from church because of her and the events of the other night.

It certainly hadn't kept Todd away.

He was already camped out in the center of the third row—right behind her usual spot every Sunday. Though he was studying the church bulletin as if it contained the great secrets of God's universe, Hannah was convinced she could see him smirking.

"Brendan's looking especially nice today," Steffie whispered after they passed him on their way to the front of the church.

He was also looking taken, given the presence of the striking blonde gripping his hand, but Hannah noticed his deep blue dress shirt and slightly darker tie for Steffie's sake. "Blue is definitely his color."

"It brings out his eyes."

Unfortunately for Steffie, she'd only had eyes for Brendan since junior high, and he'd only thought of her as a friend.

"Well, Olivia's here bright and early on this first Sunday of Advent," Steffie whispered.

As glad as she was that they were finished talking about Brendan, Hannah wished Steffie hadn't switched to that topic. "Now be nice."

Still, she couldn't resist taking a peek at Olivia Wells. Every Sunday for the last six months, Olivia had sat in coiffed blond perfection on the aisle end of the second row that marked her position as the widower minister's lady friend. The attractive widow had dressed in one of her trademark prim suits—this time red for the holiday season—and her makeup was flawless as always.

"As nice as *she* is?" Steffie asked.

"Nicer."

That wasn't fair, and Hannah knew it. Maybe she wasn't the woman Hannah would have chosen for her father, but still she had to admit that Olivia had been perfectly pleasant to her and Rebecca as well as the rest of the congregation. Because she felt guilty for suggesting otherwise, she stopped to greet Olivia warmly and gave her hand an extra squeeze before slipping past her to the center of the pew.

"Do you think she and your dad will get married?" Steffie whispered once they'd taken their seats.

"I don't know what I think."

Both became quiet as the service began, but her answer to Steffie's question continued to roll through her thoughts. It felt like the most honest thing she'd said all day and for reasons beyond her father's romantic life. Her equilibrium was as fragile as blown glass, susceptible to shattering into tiny shards with the littlest provocation.

Just over her shoulder was the man whom she couldn't seem to escape lately, when once she'd wished away the ocean that had divided them. He'd told her he wouldn't make it easy to cut him out of her life again, and his methods might have been unconventional, but he'd been doing just what he said.

The question at this point wasn't whether he would continue trying; it was why Hannah was trying so hard to prevent him from keeping his word. Why was she fighting so determinedly against what she knew in her heart to be right? Rebecca deserved the chance to know her father.

But then this wasn't about Rebecca, and she knew it. Fear paralyzed her every thought, tainted her every move. What was she afraid of? That she would feel guilty every time she saw Todd and Rebecca together? That he would love her again? Or that he wouldn't?

Hannah managed to make it through the opening hymn and the offertory, singing the notes even if their message couldn't penetrate the guilt and uncertainty crowding her heart. But as Reverend Bob stepped to the lectern, she straightened in her seat and concentrated on the sermon. Since Hannah's childhood, the melodic sound of her father's voice had always made her feel God's presence. She really needed to feel it today.

Reverend Bob began his usual first Sunday of Advent sermon on preparations for the birth of Jesus. "When Gabriel appeared to Mary to tell her that she'd been chosen to give birth to God's son, how did she respond? Did she say, 'Not now, God, I'm betrothed to this really great guy, and an unexplained pregnancy will mess up my plans'?

"No, she answered in Luke 1:38, 'Behold, I am the handmaid of the Lord; let it be to me according to your word.' Her dutiful answer becomes even more amazing when we consider several biblical scholars' assertions, based on cultural norms of the period, that Mary was probably only a girl of about thirteen at the time."

Though Hannah was certain her father had included that information in his sermons before, that detail suddenly struck her. Jesus's mother had been younger than Hannah had been when she'd delivered Rebecca.

She could just imagine the disapproving glances—Hannah remembered a few of those, as well—that Mary must have faced though she wasn't guilty of any sin. And the fear—had Mary been afraid about becoming a mother first and then the mother of God's only son?

"Did Mary hesitate, though in her time a man who found his betrothed to be with child from another man could easily have had her stoned?" Reverend Bob continued and then paused, shaking his head. "No, she simply submitted to God's will. She was an example to all of us. How will we answer when God asks something of us?"

Hannah swallowed. The words seemed to speak to

her alone. What would she do? Would she stop and act or keep running? Until now, it had always been easier to run, but she was tired. Bone tired. Now she only needed to find the strength to do what God had been telling her to do all along.

Hannah drove into the nearly empty parking lot at Hickory Ridge Church, surprised that her father had demanded a meeting with her on a Thursday night and commanded her to ask Mary Nelson to babysit Rebecca. As a rule, Reverend Bob never demanded or commanded anything, rather made suggestions and let the Lord do the rest.

She pulled to a stop under one of the streetlamps that cast a yellow haze over piles of plowed snow on the parking lot's perimeter. With daylight saving time in full force, those lights were already illuminating a midnight sky at just after the dinner hour.

Leaning her forehead on the steering wheel, Hannah took a deep breath and prayed a quick plea for fortification. Dad had probably put together the puzzle about Todd, and now he would expect to hear the truth from her. Just like Todd, her father had deserved to know everything years ago, but that didn't make facing this conversation any easier.

At the sound of a car engine, Hannah lifted her head and caught sight of another pair of headlights. She glanced to Reverend Bob's regular parking place near the main entry, but the black sedan he'd been driving for years was already there. A mini SUV pulled into the parking space next to hers. It wasn't until the driver opened the door and light flooded the interior that she recognized him.

"Not now. Not now." She threw open the door and stepped out into the slushy snow.

The subject of her frustration climbed out, as well, and waved a gloved hand as he closed his car door.

She marched around the car to face him, lifting on her toes to look larger than her usual five feet two. "Okay, I get it that you're not going away. Will you stop following me already? Stalking is a crime in Michigan."

Todd only smiled as he pulled his stocking cap down over his ears. "Really? I'll be sure to keep that in mind."

"And I know the Milford Police Chief, too."

"Oh, you mean Pete Conyers. Saw him at the Rite Aid yesterday. What are the odds that we would both run out of toothpaste the same night?"

Hannah frowned. Of course, Todd knew Pete. He'd been a young cop in the village while Todd and Hannah were still at Milford High. She would have trumped his comment by saying her good friend was a State Police trooper, but Todd would only have said how nice it was to meet Brett Lancaster when Todd had moved his church membership to Hickory Ridge on Sunday.

With a sigh, she asked, "What are you doing here, Todd?"

"It's a command appearance." He raised an eyebrow, lifting the same side of his mouth with it. "You?"

Hannah didn't even answer him. She turned away and squeezed her eyes shut instead. She'd always thought of her father as a purposeful man, a man of God who had clear-cut views on sin and consequences, but she'd never before thought of him as cruel. Was Dad really going to make her confess everything in front of Todd?

Because her eyes were burning as she opened them, she didn't turn back to Todd but trudged to the main church entrance. Footsteps crunched behind her.

Reverend Bob met her at the door.

"Hannah, you're looking lovely." He bent to drop a kiss on top of her hat-covered head. "I trust that Rebecca is doing well."

You saw her yourself at Wednesday prayer meeting, Hannah was tempted to point out, but she doubted it would do anything to make this conversation more comfortable. Why didn't he just forget all the niceties and get on with the interrogation?

As Todd came in the door behind her, Reverend Bob greeted him with a handshake. "Todd, it's good to see you again. I hope you're settling in well at the Proving Grounds."

"You know how new jobs go, Reverend. The learning curve is pretty steep right now, but hopefully I'll get to the bend before long."

Bob laughed at his comment as he pulled the glass door behind Todd into place and turned the lock. "Are you at least getting to take the new prototype cars for a spin on the test track?"

"I might eventually, but I haven't yet. As a test engineer, most of my work is using a computer to monitor data about things like temperature and voltage as the vehicle is operated under various conditions."

"Well I hope you get to test-drive one eventually." Hannah's father patted Todd on the shoulder of his heavy coat—just a mutual admiration society. She'd stepped outside of reality, Hannah decided. Whatever happened to her father toting a shotgun or whatever dads did to defend their daughters' honor?

Finally, Hannah had had enough. "Dad, what are we all doing here?"

The minister turned back to her, his expression carefully blank. "Todd thought the two of you might have some things to talk about."

Hannah shot a venomous look at Todd. "Command appearance, huh?"

"Your father set the time and the place."

"I guess it wasn't enough that you hired Harold Lasbury—my boss—as your new accountant on Friday when there are three CPA offices in Milford. Then you moved your membership to Hickory Ridge on Sunday, made an appearance at Faith Singles United on Tuesday and attended Wednesday prayer meeting last night."

Todd shrugged without remorse. "Guess not."

"I can't imagine what would have been enough."

Todd had even asked Harold if Hannah could personally handle his tax return, and he'd managed to somehow be at Breen's IGA the night she stopped in for milk, eggs and that popping rice cereal Rebecca loved so much.

It was as if he'd been watching her every move, waiting for a chance to pounce, and now he'd made her father an accomplice in his plans to get under her skin. Well, he was there, and his presence itched.

"By the way," he asked, "don't you ever go to the post office or the video store or the library?"

He met her frown with an amused expression that had her hands fisted at her sides.

"How dare you follow me! You're stalking me! What right do you have to invade my life like that?"

Todd stretched up and towered over her. "What right do you have to keep me away from my daughter?"

Hannah's retort died on her lips at Todd's announcement, and she turned wide-eyed to face her father. Reverend Bob didn't wear the compassionate minister's expression she'd come to expect from him. His was the face of a furious father.

"Enough," he said in an even voice but with enough finality to strike silence on the other two people in the room. "I need to see both of you in my office immediately."

Chapter Six

Without another word, Reverend Bob turned and strode to the stairway leading to his second-floor office. The look Todd captured her with had to be as cold as the one Hannah had trained on him, but both looked away quickly and headed in the direction the minister had taken.

When they reached his office, Hannah's father was already seated in his executive chair. He gestured to the pair of chairs opposite his desk. Never before this moment had Hannah felt her father's disappointment in such a profound way, even on that awful day when she'd had to air her humiliation in front of the whole Deacons' board.

"Dad, I'm so sorry—" Hannah began as she stiffly lowered into the chair, but her father raised his hand to stop her.

"I'm sure there's a lot of blame and guilt and apologies to go around." He first trapped Todd and then Hannah in his direct gaze.

Hannah stiffened but couldn't look away from her father. Would his disappointment spoken aloud be worse than his silent displeasure? Without looking at Todd, she sensed that he sat as straight as she did, his hands gripping the chair's arms.

"But that's not why the three of us are together tonight, is it?" He paused, crossing his arms over his chest. "We're here because of your daughter, and Rebecca deserves better than this."

Hannah opened her mouth to say something, anything, but the words wouldn't come. The thoughts wouldn't even come. She hated it that Todd found his voice first.

"I know you're right, but—"

"Todd." Reverend Bob's voice held the warning of a man—even a man of God—whose patience had worn thin. "Both of you have had plenty of chances to talk. Now it's time for you to listen."

With a curt nod, Todd sat back in the chair and rested his hands in his lap. Hannah settled back, as well, trying her best to relax when her thoughts and pulse were racing at competing speeds.

"You two are behaving like children, especially you, Hannah." He paused to focus pointedly on his daughter, making her squirm. "You are children no longer."

She straightened in her seat again, glancing sidelong at Todd. He sat stiffly, but he nodded, his Adam's apple shifting. Was this the uncomfortable way he would have looked if he and Hannah had faced her father together when she first learned of her pregnancy? She suspected the discomfort would have been the same, but she would never know how that confrontation might have gone or where the four of them might have been today.

"Selfishness is a privilege of youth," Bob began again, as if he was gearing up for one of his best sermons. But a small smile appeared where his tight expression had rested. "You two lost that privilege when you made a child together. God has entrusted Rebecca into your care, and your daughter's needs must always come first."

Hannah couldn't help shaking her head. "But Dad, I do put Rebecca first. She's everything to me."

"I know you love your daughter. I see that every day. But in this instance, you've been very selfish. This child needs a father. You know how she longs for someone to fill that role in her life."

Her breath hitched because she did know. Her sitter, Mary Nelson, occasionally repeated parts of conversations she'd overheard between Rebecca and Max Williams, who'd lost his father to an accident and then found a great stepfather in Brett Lancaster. Rebecca had been asking questions about her father long before she'd overheard Todd and Grant batting around her paternity like a weapon.

Since that horrible night, Rebecca had been asking even more difficult questions: "Why don't some daddies live with their kids?" and "Why are some mommies and daddies mad at each other?" How could Hannah explain anything to her daughter when her thoughts were muddy waters that refused to clear?

Because she didn't answer, Reverend Bob continued. "Unlike some unfortunate unwed mothers, you have a young man who is interested in, even adamant about, taking responsibility for his child. No matter what your feelings are regarding Todd, you must put them aside and allow Rebecca to have a relationship with her father."

The minister stopped then, as if he'd said his piece. Hannah let her gaze fall to her gripped hands. He was right, of course, but that didn't make it any easier to accept.

After five years of fighting for every miniscule amount of self-sufficiency, it wouldn't be easy to hand over part of the responsibility for Rebecca's care to anyone, let alone Todd. At the thought of him, Hannah couldn't help glancing his way. Todd had his gaze trained on her, a tight expression on his lips.

"And you, Todd."

At the sound of Reverend Bob's voice, both turned back to face him.

"You could have approached this situation with a lot more maturity, as well."

Todd sat forward in his chair and gripped the edge of the desk. "Now wait a minute. I tried everything—"

"Should everything have included the post office, video store and the library?" he asked, repeating Todd's own admission that he'd staked out those places.

"I suppose not."

"You suppose then that following my daughter everywhere she went wasn't the best idea?"

The side of Hannah's mouth pulled up at the sight of Todd facing her father's questions. It was just like Reverend Bob to call each of them out on the carpet by turns.

"No, not the best," Todd said, shaking his head. "But I was desperate. Five years of planning, of taking the right classes, of imagining apologies, of predicting possible outcomes and of praying, just so I could come back to…here."

Hannah blinked. It wasn't so much what he'd said, although the words he'd spoken aloud were shocking enough. But what she suspected he'd almost said was even more disquieting. *Her.* He'd done all those things, not to come back *here* but to *her.* Even though it was much too late to consider "what might have beens," she couldn't help feeling a begrudging respect for his effort. When she glanced up at her father, she caught him studying her. Had Dad read the confusion, or, worse yet, the respect, in her expression?

Without commenting on anything he'd seen, Reverend Bob turned back to Todd.

"You could have contacted me sooner." He waited for Todd's nod before he added, "Just as you could have come to me five years ago, when my daughter first locked you out of her life…and your daughter's life."

"You knew!" Hannah's question came out as a shriek, and she didn't even care. She stared at him, incredulous that her father could have kept a secret like that. Better, obviously, than she'd kept hers.

"I would tell you that fathers aren't as oblivious as

you think, but I have to admit the hints were hard to miss," he said, as he leaned forward, resting his elbows on his desk. "First, your best friend moved across the globe, and you didn't hear from him. Ever. Then you started rushing to beat me to the mailbox, even when your morning sickness was so bad you could barely get out of bed.

"And finally, I picked up my bedroom extension and heard a familiar voice and the sound of you hanging up the phone on him. I didn't even need to see Rebecca to confirm what I already knew."

"But you never said anything," Hannah said.

"What was I supposed to say?"

Todd looked back and forth between the two of them, amazed that both could so easily miss the point. "Oh, I don't know. Perhaps you could have insisted that she tell the baby's father, or at the very least you could have told me yourself."

He still couldn't get over the fact that Reverend Bob had known all along. No wonder he hadn't gone ballistic when Todd, finally desperate after trying everything else, had gone to him, confessed that he was Rebecca's father and begged for help in reaching Hannah.

"I was waiting."

"For what? Rebecca's high school graduation?" Todd's voice grew louder with each word, but he couldn't seem to be able to contain his anger. Bob, Andrew, Serena—everyone, it seemed—knew but him, and no one had bothered to give him a simple heads-up.

The noise Reverend Bob made sounded like a chuckle, but his expression held no mirth.

"I deserve that. But I was waiting until I wasn't so angry anymore. No matter how hard I tried, I couldn't be neutral in this situation. I'm Hannah's father. I was furious. It was hard to feel any obligation to the young man who stole my daughter's innocence and her childhood."

Todd gripped the side of the desk as old guilt reemerged from beneath the surface of his anger. "That wasn't fair."

"I never said it was, but it was human." Reverend Bob leaned back in his chair and crossed his arms again. "Don't get me wrong. I wasn't blaming you alone, Todd. If I remember correctly from my marriage, sexual intimacy requires two partners."

The skin on the back of Todd's neck suddenly became hot. Were they really discussing such private matters with Hannah sitting next to them? In his peripheral vision, he could see her shifting in her seat.

Reverend Bob waved his hand as if to brush away that topic as water under the bridge. "But the reason I didn't tell you was more than my anger about sin and the consequences it had on my daughter's life or even on behalf of my grandchild, who wouldn't know the security of a loving two-parent family. I was waiting for one of you to take responsibility."

"You've got to be kidding, Dad." This time Hannah came out of her seat and paced toward the window, where the cloudy night sky stretched in endless blackness, striped with gray. When she turned back to them, her hands were fisted at her sides, but her eyes appeared damp.

"For five years, I've done nothing *but* take responsibility. I've diapered and burped and laundered and skipped sleep to study so I could support my family. I've earned a bachelor's degree in less than four years and have begun my one-year apprenticeship period in public accounting so I can take the CPA exam."

Reverend Bob studied his steepled hands before he met her gaze and spoke again. "Hannah dear, if you had owned up to *all* of your responsibilities, then we wouldn't be having this conversation right now."

Her shoulders drooping, Hannah returned to her chair and slumped into it. She pressed her lips together as if she wanted to say more, but she wisely held back. It wasn't an argument she could win, anyway, just as Todd could no longer continue to play the victim. He could have done just as the minister had suggested, moving past his fear and embarrassment over their sin and asking her father to intercede for him with Hannah. His cowardice had cost him more than he'd even known.

When father and daughter continued to eye each other in a silent standoff, Todd couldn't help but to speak up. "I'm sorry it took so long." At Hannah's surprised expression, he continued, "Sorry for both of us. And for all of us."

For several long seconds, she said nothing, but then she nodded almost imperceptibly, the tiniest motion for what had to feel like a huge act of surrender. Hope, as fragile as a seedling sinking its roots in sandy soil, threatened to find a place in Todd's heart, but he was careful to contain it. He could hope for a relationship with his child and nothing more.

Reverend Bob brushed his hands together to suggest the matter was settled.

"Now that we're all on the same page, let's discuss a few things about Rebecca." He leaned forward and rested his elbows on the desk. "As Todd mentioned when he came to me, he would like to establish paternity through the courts so he can set up a plan to pay child support. If I'm correct that will mean submitting to a paternity test. Hannah, will you allow Rebecca to be tested?"

"Yes."

The minister nodded at her softly spoken answer and turned back to Todd. "After paternity is determined, you'll be able to set up a regular visitation schedule. I would like to recommend, though, that the two of you work out a temporary schedule right away."

Todd watched Hannah, dreading the moment when she would object. They'd come so far, and he hated to see all that progress wiped away because they were moving too quickly. He couldn't help backpedaling. "Well, maybe not right away, but—"

"No," Hannah said to stop him. "That's fine."

"Good." Reverend Bob opened his desk drawer and withdrew a pad of white paper and a pen. "Rebecca already knows Todd is her father, and she's very curious about him. I think it's time for the two of them to really get to know each other."

The tightening around his heart surprised Todd. With all of the opposition Hannah had given him, he had focused on the battle rather than just how important it had become to him to have a chance to be with his daughter. Gratitude filled him that he would receive his most precious gift weeks before Christmas.

He opened his mouth to thank the minister, but Hannah spoke first.

"I agree." She paused as if the next words came hard for her. "She needs to know her father."

Reverend Bob watched from his upstairs office window as his daughter and the young man who had broken her heart entered their cars and turned on the engines. Hannah and Todd might have agreed to a truce for their child's sake, but they hadn't made any grand gestures of civility as they left the building.

What had he expected, that they would shake hands and be talking again in "friendspeak"—that combination of half-finished sentences and inside jokes that had marked their friendship in their teens? As a minister, he'd been in the heart-healing business too long to believe in Pollyanna thoughts like that. Healing took time, work and a whole lot of conversations with God.

As the cars backed out of the parking places, Bob's chest tightened. He pressed his fingers into the achy place and then moved his hands to rub his temples. His body seemed to be telling him he'd just made a big mistake in getting involved in the situation between Todd and Hannah. His mind had announced the same thing the minute he'd agreed to participate with Todd in this intervention.

At least they'd agreed to seek further counseling with Andrew instead of him. Too close to the situation, he felt incapable of providing an unbiased opinion. Even agreeing to help Todd in the first place had felt like conspiring with the enemy.

Bob shook his pounding head and kneaded his aching shoulder as he returned to his desk and settled in his well-worn executive chair. That young man wasn't the enemy any more than Todd alone was to blame for what had happened between himself and Hannah. Todd had even proven his integrity as a man by his determination to be a good father to his child, despite Hannah's unwillingness to let him.

Still, there was a difference between recognizing that Todd had grown into a decent man and encouraging Hannah to let him back into her life and into her daughter's life. Bob should have protected his own child in the first place. He should have—

Bob tried to stop himself from listing again the parental failures that he'd enumerated so many times before. The series of what-ifs when history and circumstances had made them moot. If he'd been there more for her. If he'd been able to see past his own grief to help Hannah face hers. If his wife hadn't died.

"Oh, Deborah, why'd you have to leave so soon?" His words came on a sigh. He continued whispering, as much to himself as to his wife's memory. "I feel so ill-equipped to help her sometimes. You would have known."

Turning in the chair, he glanced down at the three portraits on his desk and sought out the one with the gilded frame. The image that smiled out at him was of Deborah, the first woman he'd ever loved and the one who still held his heart. Yes, his late wife would have known what to say to their daughter during the dark times over the last few years. She would have directed Hannah with her quiet dignity and inherent grace.

His gaze lingered on Deborah's smiling face and then moved to the other portraits: Hannah and Rebecca. Would Olivia's face ever look out at him from a frame on this desk? Would there come a time when he would put away Deborah's photo as a sign of his moving forward? He shrugged. Maybe not today, but perhaps one day soon.

If he did decide to move on and choose a wife, Olivia was the kind of woman who would make any man proud. The lovely widow had so many fine qualities: from her warmness and caring spirit to her generosity and steadfast faith. He'd witnessed these qualities and more since he'd helped her to secure the job in the church office the year before.

Olivia was such a wonderful addition to the downstairs office, and to his personal life, as well. He hadn't even realized there was an empty place inside of him until she'd stepped inside to fill it. And the way she looked at him sometimes, as if he held all the answers to her questions—what middle-aged man's ego wouldn't glory in that?

Would he ever be able to love Olivia, or any woman, the way he'd loved Deborah? He shook his head, not only because he was convinced he couldn't but also because it wasn't a fair question to ask. If given the choice, he always would have chosen a life with Deborah, one where their years together would have been chronicled in lines on their faces and the gentle aging of their bodies. But that choice wasn't his. Deborah was gone, and a part of his heart had died with her. Still, God had a plan for him, and that meant continuing his life on earth for now.

He had told the widows and widowers of his church this so many times before. If God wished them to love again, He would open their hearts to the possibility and give them a different love, worthy of the special individual He'd sent their way. Bob wanted to believe the words he'd said were true in his own life.

Bob had noticed that Hannah hadn't warmed to Olivia the way he had hoped she would over these last months. No one could ever replace her mother, he understood that, but he didn't believe Hannah would want him to be lonely, either. Sometime soon he would have to discuss this matter with his daughter, especially if he decided to form a closer relationship with Olivia.

Maybe a discussion would be unnecessary after they had all spent Christmas together this year. Hannah would have a better chance to get to know Olivia, and his lady friend would have the opportunity to see how she might fit in the Woods family.

The Christmas dinner was Olivia's idea. He wasn't exactly at peace with the idea of having another woman cooking in Deborah's kitchen and serving at the table where Deborah had lovingly set so many wonderful holiday meals over the years. Since her death, Bob and Hannah hadn't once eaten a Christmas, Thanksgiving or Easter dinner at home, always accepting gracious invitations from other church members.

So for him, this dinner was a significant first step in his personal life. He would simply have to pray for the strength to push aside feelings that allowing someone else into his life was abandoning the memory of his wife.

Changes. There were certainly a lot of them in his family this holiday season, beyond this first Christmas dinner at home in years. For the first time since Rebecca had been born, she wouldn't wake up Christmas morning in her grandfather's home. He knew how important it was for Hannah to make this statement of her independence by spending the morning in her new apartment, but he knew how much he would miss watching Rebecca's joy as she opened her presents.

Hannah would deal with some sadness of her own, as, for the first time, Rebecca would spend at least part of the holidays with her father. If loneliness filled him at the thought of his adult daughter being away from him Christmas morning, he could just imagine how Hannah would feel without her child.

Would they find a way to focus on the glory of the Christ child's birth when they were all so caught up in the drama of their own lives? Bob hoped so. He also hoped he would have the right words for Hannah if she came to him and asked his advice about dealing with Todd.

He sensed that the young man might still have feelings for his daughter, but would those feelings be enough to erase all of the pain and sorrow between them? Or would Todd's reappearance only result in more pain for all of them?

All the questions only made Bob's body ache more. He held his head in the cradle of his hands and closed his eyes. Slowly, a realization awakened in him: Why, when his world felt so heavy, had he been trying to bear it alone? Strange, if one of his church members had been feeling this same weight, he would have suggested that she turn it over to God. What made it so hard for him to follow his own advice?

Father, I'm entrusting all of these questions to Your capable hands. You've known the answers all along. Please share them with us in Your time. Amen.

As he ended his prayer, words from one of his favorite passages, Psalm 27, filtered through his thoughts. He whispered the words in the room's silence. "'The Lord is my light and my salvation; whom shall I fear? The Lord is the stronghold of my life; of whom shall I be afraid?'"

Bob felt relief for that first time since he'd called

Hannah and insisted on her presence at the church that night. Everything would be fine, he suddenly knew with certainty. The situation was safely in God's hands.

Chapter Seven

Hannah lifted her collar to block the wind, wishing she could as easily warm her insides, but that was unlikely on this night of firsts. Around the three of them, the display windows of Milford's downtown shops were dressed for the season with miniature Christmas trees, garland and twinkling lights. The wind caused the outdoor displays to jiggle and sway as if adding its own layer to the season's air of anticipation. Christmas was only nine days away.

Strange how all of that gaiety seemed distant to Hannah, as if she was extraneous to it, just as she was to tonight's father-daughter outing. Though she understood that this was a good thing, she couldn't help feeling as if she was looking at Todd and Rebecca from outside the glass.

Todd had suggested that Hannah join him and Rebecca on their first outing, even though she'd been at home both times he'd visited in the last week. He thought Rebecca might be more comfortable with Hannah there, and she'd agreed. Now if she had to spend the night walking on eggshells—or crunching over snow on Main Street as the case appeared to be—she would do what it took to make the night go smoothly for her daughter.

Still, needing something to do with her fidgety hands, Hannah reached down to pull up Rebecca's hood, but her daughter picked that moment to race ahead. The child's unzipped red parka flapped behind her like the cape of "Amazing Rebecca," out to save humanity once again.

"Look at me. Look at me."

Hannah was looking, all right, and choking back mom panic regarding slippery ice, strangers and fast-moving cars. "Rebecca, slow down."

Oblivious to the danger, Rebecca looked back at them and ran even faster, past shoppers with armloads of packages and lighted trees in the downtown side-walks. Hannah shot a worried glance Todd's way, but he only gave her a mischievous grin before shooting out after their daughter.

"You can't escape me," he called in his best monster imitation as he captured Rebecca in his arms. He swung her around and around, eliciting giggles though he had effectively ended her escape. When they finally stopped spinning, Todd lowered the dizzy child to the ground and knelt in front of her to zip her coat.

"It's cold out. You need to keep this zipped." He pulled her hood up over her ponytails and then dug her mittens from her pockets and slipped them over her hands.

Amazingly, Rebecca didn't even fight his efforts, though as an independent preschooler, she usually refused all assistance with winter wear on principle. Todd appeared more like a relaxed veteran than the inexperienced father he was. His ministrations lacked the efficiency of movement Hannah had learned with four years of practice, but what he lost in style, he made up for in humor. Finally finished, he stood and patted Rebecca's head.

"There. Now doesn't that feel warmer?"

Taking her hand, he strode back to where Hannah stood watching them. He glanced down at the child looking up at him. "You don't want to scare your mother again by running off like that. You could fall on the ice or get hit by one of those cars. They go really fast."

Hannah couldn't help smiling at the back of his head as Todd stood and turned away from her. *Scare your mother.* Rebecca had worried one of her parents, all right, but for this one, the experience was new and intense.

"Okay, Daddy. Can we look at the toy store now?"

They'd stopped in front of the Village Toy Shoppe's brightly decorated display window, but no one except the child took notice. Hannah's breath caught. *Daddy.* The new title flowed so naturally from Rebecca's lips. How quickly she'd adapted to Todd's arrival and his new place in her life. Todd had heard it, too. Hannah could tell by how stiffly he stood. He glanced sidelong at Hannah, his eyes a little too shiny in the streetlamp's glow.

Hannah's own eyes burned as she lowered her gaze to the child standing between them. If bliss had a face, it would have been the one looking up at her. A wave of emotion rolled over Hannah, the last of her reluctance floating back to sea with the frothy tide. This was the right thing for Rebecca.

"Can we go?" Rebecca repeated, drawing her eyebrows together.

"Of course we can look," Hannah answered when it appeared Todd wasn't ready. She used the same phrasing she always used when the two of them entered toy stores. Browsing was usually all the two of them could fit into the budget, except for Christmas and birthdays, and even then extravagant gifts were out of the question.

They took a few steps toward the entrance of the small mall where the toy store was housed.

"Wait." Todd stopped and turned to Rebecca. "Does this mean you think you might be getting toys sometime soon?"

Rebecca giggled again. "Santa brings me toys for Christmas…if I'm good."

"Oh, really? You're probably good all the time then."

Her tinkling little-girl laughter flitted through the crisp air.

"Most of the time, anyway," Hannah assured him.

"Then let's hurry. We have a lot of toys to pick out."

"Mommy says it's not nice to ask for too many. God and Santa wouldn't like that."

The side of Hannah's mouth pulled up. At least her daughter had mentioned God first. She didn't mind Rebecca enjoying the fantastical celebrations at Christmas as long as she knew the real reason for the season.

Todd swung Rebecca's arm as he started again toward the shopping center's door. "Your mom's right. You don't want to be greedy. But that doesn't mean we can't look at every single toy before you pick a few special ones to put on your Christmas list."

"Will you look at *every single toy,* too?"

"Absolutely. I love toys." Todd glanced back over his shoulder. "What about you, Mommy? Are you ready to look at more toys than any kid should own?"

"I'm right behind you." Hannah shook her head, but she couldn't help smiling at the merry prattling of her companions about baby dolls, race cars, plastic dinosaurs and building sets as they stepped inside the mall entrance and continued into the specialty toy shop.

Rebecca and her father were so at ease with each other, no longer strangers, as they'd been a week before, but fast friends. They seemed to share a comfortable, private rhythm, a sign that they were building a foundation for a relationship between just the two of them.

Hannah waited, expecting jealousy to squeeze inside her and to strangle all the magnanimous feelings she'd been experiencing tonight. Todd was an interloper; before, Rebecca's heart had belonged to her mother alone.

To her surprise, Hannah felt only warmth. Her eyes were wet as she stared at the blur of bright colors from games, toys and puzzles stacked high in the tiny shop.

Strange how she didn't feel cramped herself in this new relationship. There seemed to be plenty of room for both Todd and her in Rebecca's heart.

She'd been naive to believe Rebecca didn't need a father in her life. Now she wanted that for her daughter. It had become intrinsically tied to all the hopes and dreams Hannah had for her child: for a strong relationship with God, for a good education, for love, adventure, dreams and joy.

"Mommy?"

Hannah glanced down at the little love of her life, who was pulling on the hem of her parka to get her attention. A packaged collector's doll in a satiny pink dress rested in her daughter's arms.

"Do you think Santa would mind if I asked for just one doll this year?"

"Sweetie, that isn't really the kind of doll that you would play with." Or one her mother could afford. That familiar disappointment pulled at her spirit, a reminder of the way that tight budgets warred with Hannah's need for independence in caring for her child.

"But she opens and shuts her eyes and everything." The child shifted the box to demonstrate before hugging the package to her chest.

"She sure does, but this doll—" Hannah paused to read the name printed on the box "—Miss Gabrielle is the kind of toy you put up on your shelf to look pretty."

"She is pretty, Mommy. Look, her hair's just like Tessa's."

Hannah glanced down at the doll's collection of

dark curls, all tidily collected with a bright pink ribbon. That hair would look *exactly* like Tessa's unruly mass of springy curls before they could finish Christmas breakfast.

"You mean Andrew and Serena's little girl?" Todd asked as he came closer to study the doll.

"She's a big girl. Tessa's nine."

"Ooh, I stand corrected," Todd said seriously.

"But the doll…" Hannah began again.

"Okay, Mommy. I'll put her back." Rebecca returned the toy to the shelf with her sister pricey dolls but only after several hugs and a promise to visit. Even after Miss Gabrielle was standing tall next to her sisters, Rebecca stood looking up at her with longing.

Hannah peeked over at Todd, who appeared to be fighting back a smile and losing the battle. He crooked his index finger to call Hannah over to him. Her stance stiffened. He wasn't going to question her parenting, was he? She jumped in before he had the chance.

"Look, Todd, no child should ever have everything she wants. Even if I could afford it." She glanced around, hoping Rebecca hadn't overheard, and lowered her voice. "I've had to explain this to Dad and to my child-care provider, Mary, but I don't want everyone overindulging Rebecca. They need to understand that I'm the parent."

"Rebecca has two parents now," Todd pointed out softly.

Hannah blew out an exasperated sigh. "I know, but…" She let the words trail off because even she didn't know but *what*. Todd kept a solemn expression when he could have given her the condescending smile she deserved. She appreciated that.

"I know I'm new at this parenting thing, but I just want to be a part of the team, okay?" He squeezed her shoulder and released it quickly.

"I promise not to buy things for Rebecca every time I take her anywhere. And I won't ply her with treats. Buying someone's love dooms a relationship as much as it does a wallet."

Hannah's body relaxed from the battle that would be unnecessary. Rebecca continued to stare at the doll, having a tough time saying goodbye to her dream. At least this coparenting thing might not be as difficult as Hannah had first imagined.

Todd was a reasonable person. She'd forgotten that about him. His reasonableness had been one of the things she'd liked about him. One of many.

"That said," Todd began, but stared into her eyes as if gauging her reaction before he continued, "it's Christmas. Can *our* daughter, this one time, have something utterly impractical, just because her daddy wants to indulge her?"

Again, that word. *Daddy*. Images of Hannah with her own father flooded her mind. But those memories of normal activities—of unwrapping presents and removing training wheels—transformed into stark thoughts of a teenage girl and her father standing next to a casket in the snow.

Todd tilted his head to the side and studied her quizzically when she didn't answer. "Please, Hannah."

Hannah was weakening—she could feel it, but that didn't stop her from pressing her argument once more. "You saw it. That doll is ridiculously expensive."

He nodded, his gaze never leaving hers. "Ridiculously. And Rebecca will want to play with it instead of leaving it on a shelf to collect dust. Miss Gabrielle will probably be naked and have messy hair before Christmas day is even over."

When she glanced at him sharply, Todd shrugged.

"I've seen her other dolls. She seems to prefer them au naturel."

"If you know it's too expensive and even that she won't care for it the way she should, then why do you still want to buy it for her?"

"It's my first Christmas as a dad. I want to make it special."

Hannah had opened her mouth to try again, but her teeth clicked shut. Her heart squeezed. For the last few weeks, she'd thought only how their lives—hers and Rebecca's—had changed. Todd's life had been altered just as dramatically, and yet he was relishing the newness. No matter what the difficult circumstances of her birth, Rebecca was blessed to have a father like Todd.

"I'm sure she'll be pleased," Hannah said finally. "When would you plan to give it to her?"

Todd sent a quick glance Rebecca's way and then turned his sheepish expression on Hannah. "Well, I've already bought a few Christmas presents for her—just a few books, games and stuff. I wouldn't want to give her too many presents, so I was hoping that this one could be a present she finds under the tree Christmas morning. From Santa."

From Mommy and Daddy, he might as well have said. How easily he'd bypassed the delicate subject of affordability. As much as she appreciated that, she didn't want his thoughtfulness to go unrewarded.

"Are you sure you don't want her to know? Each time she plays with the doll, she would remember that it was a gift from you. She'd know you were thinking of her."

"That doesn't matter." He glanced up as a very solemn Rebecca made her way back to them. "I just want to see her smile."

"Look at this one, Mommy."

In her palm, Rebecca proudly held up a tiny star-shaped sugar cookie. Well, it was almost a star, though one of its five points was missing, and the remaining four were far from even.

"That's really nice, honey." Hannah bent to brush some of the flour off her daughter's face. She didn't know why she bothered. Only a bath could remove all the batter, frosting and colored-sugar sprinkles that had decorated Rebecca along with the cookies.

"Nice? Nice, you say?" Todd wore an incredulous expression as he looked up from the table where he and Rebecca sat, cutting the shapes and putting them on baking sheets. "Now that cookie is amazing."

Setting his own cookie cutter aside, Todd moved the

newest creation from Rebecca's hand to the pan among the other stars, Christmas trees and Santa shapes. On his black turtleneck and black jeans, he wore nearly as much flour and sprinkles as his daughter did. Hannah's fingers itched to grab her camera again, but she'd already taken several pictures, and even Rebecca was sick of posing.

"What color frosting are you going to put on it after it's baked?" Todd asked her. "Green, white or red?"

Rebecca squinted and studied the cookie for several seconds before coming to a decision. "Blue."

Todd nodded as if seeing the finished masterpiece the way Rebecca envisioned it. "Blue sounds great."

"You mean we need to make *more* frosting?" Hannah put on her best stern expression when she asked it. Really, she didn't mind a bit that they would use up all the flour, confectioner's sugar and food coloring in the house and that she would be scrubbing cookie dough off the tabletop, cabinet doors and laminate kitchen floor for days.

"More frosting. Yum!"

"You were right, Becca." Todd nuzzled his messy little girl under his chin. "This was a better idea than sledding."

She poked his nose playfully and squirmed out of his grasp. "You wanted to make cookies, Daddy."

"But you were the one who thought it sounded like fun."

Hannah swallowed a chuckle as she took the three-step walk back to the counter where she'd been whipping frosting of various colors. She'd suspected that cookie making had been Todd's idea, but now they'd confirmed it. Rebecca and her father could have gone sledding together as they had on Sunday, but he'd made a point of including Hannah this time in the fun. Gratitude filled her that he had. Maybe someday she would learn to enjoy the solitude while her daughter spent time with her father, but at this point, the apartment felt too empty, her heart too lonely.

To keep her hands busy, Hannah pulled her last mixing bowl from the cabinet and measured one-third cup of butter for her fourth recipe of buttercream frosting.

Rebecca must have recognized that the new project left the other bowls unattended because she slipped over to the counter, pulled a bowl down to her level and scooped a dollop of green frosting with her finger. She had that finger in her mouth before Hannah could turn off the mixer.

"Rebecca Faith Woods." Hannah pretended to threaten her child with the business end of a rubber spatula and earned a round of giggles for her trouble.

Todd glanced over from the table, but his mouth was tight. At first, his reaction confused Hannah until she realized she'd spoken their daughter's last name aloud. That name wasn't McBride.

She was beginning to imagine how uncomfortable that had to make Todd and how important it would be to him for his child to carry his name. Hannah met his gaze and smiled at him tremulously, hoping it reassured him. The name would be another thing they would discuss in the weeks to come.

Todd smiled back at her, and the strangest thing happened. Oh, she remembered it, all right. Knees like gelatin without a proper mold. Pulse pounding out a Latin beat. With Todd, she'd felt this strange sensation so many times—a tickling electricity, a sense of being more fully alive. In the last five years, she hadn't felt anything like it.

Not until Todd came back.

Hannah drew in a sharp breath that she covered by clearing her throat. As a distraction, she flipped the mixer back on and whipped the butter until it was fluffy.

But the spinning beaters only seemed to underscore the thoughts whirling through her mind. When had her anger against him cooled? When had she come to see him as anything besides an obstacle to her independent life with her child? She couldn't say. More disconcerting than that, now that the first of these unacceptable thoughts had escaped her tight hold, she couldn't make them stop.

As if he was unaware of the battle of wills inside Hannah and the wide berth he should give her because of it, Todd leaned close and nabbed the container of red frosting off the countertop.

He shrugged when Hannah batted her spatula at him. "I have to make sure the red tastes okay, too." He popped a fingerful into his mouth and made a humming sound of approval low in his throat.

"It's good, isn't it, Daddy?" Rebecca said.

Hannah grabbed the bowl of white frosting before either of them decided to double-dip with their germ-covered fingers. She frowned at Todd.

"Some example you are."

Perhaps he wasn't a great example for healthy baking techniques, but he was a really good dad. He seemed to have donned the role so easily, and he wore it well. In one side of the strong, confident man he'd become, Todd had maintained a childlike sense of play and an ability to laugh at himself.

Hannah couldn't help watching him with Rebecca, as he laughed genuinely at jokes from a four-year-old and made a game out of creating the ugliest cookies ever. In a tender moment, he brushed Rebecca's gummy hair back from her face, the flour on his hands only adding to the mess.

"I do my best."

Hannah shot a sidelong glance at him as he returned to the table and helped Rebecca back into her chair. He was responding to her remark about his eating the frosting, but it almost felt as though he'd read her thoughts and had answered them instead. Without looking up, Todd rolled out another ball of sugar cookie dough. His daughter stuck a bell-shaped cutter right in the center, just as she had done the last three times, and still he laughed.

Todd covered his daughter's tiny hand with his, her fingers so dwarfed by his that they seemed to disappear. Hannah found she wasn't jealous of that special touch between father and daughter. No mother would deny her child the opportunity to smile like that.

Still, Hannah couldn't help remembering the warmth of Todd's hand when he'd covered her fingers with his own. She'd felt safe and precious in his arms. Would it ever be possible for her to be on the receiving end of his caring again? And, more importantly, would she ever want that?

Returning her attention to the bowl in front of her, Hannah mixed the confectioner's sugar into the butter and added vanilla and milk before squeezing in about half a tube of blue gel food coloring. The result was a bowl of cornflower-blue frosting—not a color she would normally have associated with Christmas.

"How many more days until Christmas, Mommy?"

Hannah took a few seconds to calculate. "Just five. It won't be long now." She smiled, knowing full well that to a four-year-old, five days was a lifetime.

"Can Daddy come to our house for Christmas?"

Hannah's cheeks grew warm. "We've already discussed this, sweetie. You're going to your daddy's apartment for dinner on Christmas Eve, and then we'll all go to the service together Christmas morning. It's Sunday this year."

She glanced at Todd, realizing suddenly that she didn't know what further plans he had. With no family around and no time to have made close friends, Todd would probably be spending the holiday alone. No one should be alone on Christmas, and her heart squeezed with the sense that Todd might be.

Rebecca was shaking her head when Hannah looked back at her. "No, Mommy. When I get up. Can Daddy come when I open my presents from Santa?"

Hannah paused, waiting for the bite of jealousy to sting. This would be their first Christmas in their own apartment. Hannah had looked forward for months to having this private morning to mark their move to independence—just the two of them. But the only thing that struck her was a sense of rightness. Of course, Todd should be there when Rebecca opened Miss Gabrielle, for so many reasons beyond his special gift.

"Sure, he can…if he wants to." After washing her hands, she wiped them on a dish towel and turned back to him. "Todd, would you like to join us for Christmas morning and breakfast before church?"

He didn't hesitate. "That sounds great."

"You could come to Christmas dinner, too, if you like. It will be at my father's. His…friend is cooking dinner."

"Thanks, but I've already agreed to have dinner with the Westins."

"Oh, you'll enjoy that. We've spent several holidays with the Westins."

Her disappointment was as quick as it was bewildering. She turned back to the sink to rinse blue frosting off the beaters. It should have come as no surprise that Andrew and Serena had extended an invitation to Todd. They usually planned a big celebration, inviting all those who might otherwise have a lonely holiday.

She was disappointed for Rebecca's sake, she tried to

tell herself. It was too difficult to admit that at least part of her frustration had nothing to do with her daughter.

Over her shoulder, Hannah found herself saying, "Well, maybe you could drop by for dessert then."

When Hannah turned back from the counter, Todd had stood up from the table and was studying her, his eyebrows drawn together. His gaze found hers and held it. So many emotions danced in his eyes, and he seemed willing to bare them all—regret, frustration and hope.

Rebecca, oblivious to the unspoken conversation, stood up, as well, and slipped her sticky hand into her father's.

"Please, Daddy. Please eat dessert with us."

Todd glanced down at her and smiled. "For you, sweetheart…anything."

Chapter Eight

Christmas dawned clear but frigid as rare winter sunshine glinted off ice-covered branches and snow-flocked evergreens. Todd didn't even mind that he could see his breath inside his car as he drove to the morning festivities at Hannah's apartment. He hadn't been this excited for Christmas morning since he was a little boy.

He had only parked his car by the curb and stepped out into the snow when Rebecca threw open the door.

"Merry Christmas, Daddy. Look, Mommy curled my hair." She shook her head, sending the cascade of tight blond ringlets flying.

"Merry Christmas. I like your hair."

"I have a new dress, too."

Rebecca spun in the doorway, making the full skirt of the velvety red dress pouf out around her.

"It's very pretty."

She wrinkled her nose. "It itches."

Before his daughter could run out into the snow and launch herself into his arms, fancy dress, black buckle shoes and all, Todd hurried up the steps. Balancing the shopping bag filled with gifts in one arm, he nabbed Rebecca and propped her on his hip.

Todd pressed his cheek to hers, breathing in the clean, baby shampoo scent that he'd come to associate with his daughter. She looked so sweet and pretty this morning. If only his parents could have come for Christmas. He would have loved to have the chance to introduce his daughter to them today, but part of him was equally glad that it was just the three of them this special Christmas morning.

"We've been waiting all morning for you, Daddy."

Todd closed the door, setting the shopping bag aside. "All morning? It's only seven-thirty."

"Yes, *all* morning," Hannah called from down the hall. Her tired voice suggested just how early Rebecca had awakened for Christmas morning.

Lowering his daughter to the floor, Todd hung his coat on the coat tree in the entry and waited. He expected to see some of that exhaustion on Hannah's face as she entered the room, but she looked serene in an elegant black dress that smoothed over her trim figure and fell nearly to her ankles. She'd worn her hair long today, the tresses turned softly toward her face, and around her neck she'd draped a strand of shimmering pearls.

Time paused for a few seconds as Todd forgot to breathe. Hannah was so beautiful. Her hair, that skin, those lips—he'd tried so hard these last four weeks not to see, not to remember. But here she stood about eight feet from him, giving him one of those smiles that used to take him down like a bat to the back of the knees. Clearly, it still could. All those feelings he'd worked so hard to bury came flooding back.

He needed to look away from her, but he couldn't help watching for a few seconds longer. Hannah continued to watch him, too, though she blushed prettily just as she had so long ago. Maybe he hadn't imagined the connection he'd thought they'd made the other night at Hannah's apartment. Maybe…no, he had no business going there. It was reckless to hope.

"Can we open presents now, Mommy? Please."

Startled, Todd and Hannah glanced down at the child now standing in the space between them, looking back and forth and wearing a confused expression.

Hannah was first to recover. "I did tell her she could open her gifts as soon as you got here."

"It's Jesus's birthday, but we get presents, too," Rebecca told him.

"Oh, really. Why do you think that is?"

Rebecca pursed her lips and squinted her eyes in concentration before answering. "Because God wants us all to have fun."

"It's really more than that," Hannah began, but then she stopped. "Maybe I should wait for a more teachable moment on that one."

"Why? Does someone want to open gifts right away?"

"I do! I do!" Rebecca chimed.

"Are you sure you don't want to wait until after

breakfast, Becca? Maybe some pancakes or eggs and bacon?"

The child's sunny expression fell. "No, thank you."

"Well, since you said it so politely…" Todd looked to Hannah for confirmation.

Instead of answering, Hannah lowered her gaze to the shopping bag by the door. "More presents?"

"I held back last night."

"Not enough when you were shopping, apparently."

"Guilty." Todd raised his hands, palms up, but he refused to be sorry. "I couldn't help myself."

"Oh, well." Hannah frowned. "Rebecca, do you want to hand out the presents?"

Their daughter didn't waste any time rushing into the living room and digging several packages from under the tree. The collection wasn't large, but Hannah had made each package special by adding curly ribbons, bows and candy canes to the bright holiday wrapping paper.

Hannah crossed the room and sat on the sofa next to her camera bag. Todd sat in the recliner opposite her.

"This is mine." Rebecca set a small package in the center of the floor before retrieving another from the tree. She went back to the tree several times and returned to add packages to her little pile.

"She's reading already?" Todd asked, his chest puffing up with fatherly pride.

"A little. They learn to recognize their names from their badges at preschool."

Glancing back from the tree, Rebecca grinned and

held out a small package wrapped in homemade paper that was covered with Christmas stamps. "This one says 'Mommy.'"

"She made that at preschool, too."

Rebecca scrambled over to hand the present to her mother and then rushed back to the tree. The next package she lifted was identical to the other. "This one says 'Daddy.'"

"Oh. Wow."

"Rebecca asked her teachers if she could make two gifts. Wasn't that nice?"

Todd could only nod. His throat became dry. His eyes burned. It wasn't as if he hadn't considered that his daughter might give him a Christmas gift, courtesy of her mother. But this was special. It was Rebecca's idea.

"Put your dad's pile right by his feet."

Having missed her father's strange reaction and her mother's effort to cover for him, Rebecca continued happily digging behind the tree and pulling out the last few packages. After asking her mother to read the name on the two final boxes, including one that she struggled to carry, Rebecca placed them next to Todd. He peeked at Hannah, who only looked away shyly.

"What about those presents?" Rebecca pointed to the bag by the door.

"How about I pass those out?" Todd stood and stepped over to the door to retrieve the bag.

The first two he placed in Rebecca's pile, and the remaining four he set at Hannah's feet.

"You weren't supposed to do this."

"Why? You did."

Her gaze fell on the two presents in Todd's pile. "Mine were just— Oh, never mind."

Twin pink spots appeared on her cheeks again, but a small smile lifted her lips, as well.

To Todd, her reaction felt like a gift in itself. This was the Hannah he remembered: the girl who got a kick out of sunsets, who could be excited about a gift box without even caring what was inside. That Hannah had been open to the world's surprises without constantly guarding herself against its pitfalls. He was so pleased to know a part of that girl remained in the woman she'd become.

"I'm youngest," Rebecca announced. "I get to go first."

When nobody argued with that, she tore into the first package. Soon the floor was littered with paper and ribbon, and a felt board play set, a princess dress-up outfit and a doll diaper bag were piled next their daughter.

Though Todd had wisely saved only the less-glamorous gifts of books and a puzzle for Christmas morning so as not to rain on Hannah's parental moment, he couldn't wait for Rebecca to choose the big package on the bottom of her stack. She saved that one for last.

"Mommy, Daddy!" she shrieked. "Santa brought Miss Gabrielle!" She hugged the doll to her, box and all, and posed for the camera with her new best friend.

"Oh, Rebecca, she's so pretty. Santa has good taste." Hannah exchanged a secretive glance with Todd and nodded her approval, as if she'd decided the doll wasn't such a bad purchase after all.

"Well, look at that." Todd realized his smile was probably bigger than even Rebecca's, but Todd didn't care. He loved seeing her this happy and knowing he'd had a part in this wonderful surprise.

Everything about his being a father had been a surprise, from the reality of it to the joy he'd found in it. He'd known Rebecca for such a short time, and yet he couldn't imagine his life without her.

Though he had no doubt she was her own person and would flex the muscles of her independence more and more as she grew, Todd was pleased to know that she demonstrated the best in both of her parents: her mother's spirit and enthusiasm and her father's dry wit. Rebecca made him proud and humbled him at the same time. God had given them all a special gift when He'd brought this child into their lives.

"Mommy, can you help me open it?"

"I just don't know why she didn't ask me for help," Todd said with a feigned frown.

"From what Rebecca told me, her new fashion doll lost most of its hair last night when you took it out of the package." Hannah knelt next to Rebecca, opened the box and made quick work of removing the plastic ties that held Miss Gabrielle captive.

He stepped behind her and examined her work over her shoulder. "Hey, you got the easier packaging. Houdini couldn't have escaped from the one I had."

Hannah straightened, taking on an air of superiority.

"Maybe I just make it look easy." She held the straight face for several seconds before it folded into a grin. "It gets easier. Really. But you've already figured that out all on your own."

After her last words, Hannah looked up at him, making it clear she meant more than just the parental headache of wrestling with toy manufacturers' packaging. She seemed to speak of parenting in general, and, unless he was mistaken, she had just encouraged him and maybe even complimented him on his growth as a dad.

Todd cleared his throat and looked away to fight the emotion building inside him. "You go next, Hannah. We have to hurry. If you don't mind, I have a story I'd like to read before breakfast."

"Sounds great."

Hannah unwrapped the giant white-chocolate candy bar, the leather-covered journal and the Detroit Pistons plaque, inserting an embarrassed "you didn't have to" right after each "thank you."

"You see? I couldn't help myself."

It had been a balancing act, choosing inexpensive gifts that wouldn't seem too personal for their tentative relationship but would be symbolic to Hannah. Todd could tell from the way she chewed her lip and didn't make eye contact with him that the favorite things of her past still meant something to her now.

As she opened the last gift, a Christmas ornament for the collection she'd been amassing since she was a little girl, Todd wondered if he'd gone too far. It was a simple glass ball ornament with a painting of the Madonna. Why hadn't he considered that the token he'd purchased as a tribute to both Hannah's late mother and the mom Hannah had become might just be a stark reminder of all she'd lost?

For a few seconds, Hannah covered her face with her hands, but then she spread them aside. Though her eyes were shining with tears, she was smiling. Pain did fade, it appeared…over time. Perhaps, just perhaps, anger faded, as well.

"Thanks, Todd." She tilted her head to the side and coughed into her hand. "That was sweet."

"It's your turn, Daddy."

Rebecca scrambled over to the pile of gifts next to him and lifted the smaller of the two packages up to him. Inside it was a navy wool scarf.

"It's to keep you warm," Rebecca explained.

"The winter's going to hit you pretty hard after a few years near the Equator." Hannah indicated with a nod of her head for their daughter to hand Todd the second, much heavier gift.

As Todd pulled a thick photo album from inside the box, he glanced over at Hannah.

"I thought you deserved your own copy of history."

On the first page were the words "Rebecca's Birth Day." In one picture, Hannah stood in a hospital gown, her hands resting on her full, rounded belly. Those that followed were the first pictures of a wrinkly and bald baby being cradled by her mother, grandfather and a woman Todd recognized from church.

A few pages further into the book, the photos began

to change. Instead of snapshots alone, there were incredible black-and-white images—of the baby sleeping under a spray of sunlight, a toddler splashing water at the beach. Todd turned a few more pages, but those obviously professional pictures continued to be mixed among the candid shots.

Remembering, Todd glanced over to the Christmas tree and the framed artistic photos on the wall behind it. He shot a glance back to Hannah.

"They're yours, aren't they? You're the photographer."

She nodded, smiling. "It's a hobby mostly. A photographer and an accountant—a strange combination, don't you think?"

"Not strange. Anyway, you're a great photographer."

"It brings in a little extra money."

He studied the framed photos again as his thoughts were drawn to another place, another time. "You used to take pictures all the time. I hated it."

He chuckled with the memory of the wrestling matches that had resulted from his efforts to remove that camera from her hands…and the embraces that usually ended the game. Hannah must have remembered, as well, because she suddenly looked away, embarrassed.

"Thank you." He waited for her to look back at him before he continued. "It's great. I love it."

"I'm glad." She cleared her throat.

"Do they have Christmas at your old house, Daddy?"

Todd glanced up from the photo album. "You mean in Singapore?" At her nod, he continued. "It's an island, you know. Some people there celebrate Christmas just like us. But they don't have snow like we have here. It's very hot, and it's rainy sometimes."

"Are they sad that there's no snow?"

A smile pulled at his lips. "Maybe some are, but many like the warm weather, too."

Her attention span filled with all the geography she could handle for one day, Rebecca turned back to her toys and immediately began undressing her doll.

"Didn't you say something about a story?" Hannah reminded Todd.

Rebecca looked up from the floor. "Yeah, Daddy, will you read us a story? Please."

"I can do that." He reached one last time into his shopping bag and produced his worn, brown-leather Bible. Opening it to the passage he'd already marked, Todd made room for Rebecca to squeeze in next to him in the recliner. "I thought this would be a perfect occasion to read from the Book of Luke. It's about Joseph and Mary's trip to Bethlehem.

"'While they were there, the time came for the baby to be born, and she gave birth to her firstborn, a son. She wrapped him in cloths and placed him in a manger, because there was no room for them in the inn.'"

"Mommy said a manger was a eating trough for animals. Why did they put Baby Jesus there?"

"Joseph and Mary were away from home and didn't have a bed for Baby Jesus. At least the hay in the manger would keep our Lord warm. There He was, the Son of God, sleeping beside the farm animals."

Todd hoped Hannah would pipe in with her opinion on the subject, but he only caught her staring at him strangely. "What? What is it?"

Instead of answering immediately, Hannah continued to stare at him, looking perplexed.

"Is something wrong, Hannah?"

She shook her head. "No, not wrong."

"Then what is it?"

"I thought I knew you so well," she said with a shrug. "I never really knew you at all, did I?"

At first her words made no sense to him, and then realization dawned. Though years ago Hannah had heard him speak of so many things, he'd never spoken so openly of his faith. Or had a whole lot of faith to speak of.

"You knew me. You still do." Though he itched to touch her hand, Todd reached out to her with his smile alone. "I've changed some. But some changes are for the better."

Chapter Nine

"Are you sure you don't want another slice of pumpkin pie, Todd?"

Olivia Wells already had the pie plate in one hand, the server poised in the other. Sitting across from Hannah at the Woods family's formal dining room table, Todd appeared almost the sage color of his sweater. He'd already eaten large servings of Olivia's apple pie, cherries jubilee and Black Forest cake, even after consuming his share of the massive Christmas dinner at the Westins'.

"Come on, Todd. One more couldn't hurt," Reverend Bob prodded, holding back a smile.

"Except that it might make me explode right here on Mrs. Wells's heirloom tablecloth."

Hannah shook her head. "Ew, that wouldn't be pretty."

"Now, Todd, didn't I tell you to call me Olivia?"

"Sorry. But no, thank you, Mrs.— I mean, Olivia.

Your desserts are amazing, but I couldn't eat another bite."

Reverend Bob pushed back from the table and patted his full belly. "I believe I've had enough, as well, though the meal was wonderful." He flashed a grateful look to Olivia before turning back to Todd. "Did you get the chance to talk to your parents today?"

"I called them this morning, which was already tonight, their time. Mom said the day was sunny and eighty-five degrees."

"Did you tell her you'd build a snowman for her?" Hannah asked.

He nodded. "She told me she'd make a sand castle at the beach for me."

"When do you think they'll return stateside?" Bob sat back with his hand pressed to his stomach.

"Dad already took an extension, so he should be returning soon. They've been talking about wanting to come back a lot lately." He didn't have to mention the current development that probably had inspired their interest in moving back soon.

"It's too bad they couldn't come just for the holiday," Bob continued. "We would have loved having them here, and I know they would have enjoyed Olivia's cooking."

Again, Bob smiled at his guest, and Olivia beamed. If this woman could make her father that happy, Hannah decided she could at least try to make an effort.

"Uh, Olivia, I just wanted to tell you that you really

outdid yourself with Christmas dinner. Thanks so much for planning this."

She meant it, too, even though initially she'd felt strange seeing her mother's good china paired with Olivia's lace tablecloth and linen napkins. The turkey had been golden and juicy, the side dishes, scrumptious. Olivia's ham with honey-apricot glaze even had finicky Rebecca returning for seconds.

Although Hannah had been uncomfortable with the idea of sharing Christmas with her father's lady friend, the celebration had been lovely. It was another great addition to the day that began with the private gift exchange at her apartment and continued through Reverend Bob's inspiring holiday sermon at church.

Olivia stood up from the table and started stacking dishes. "It's unfortunate that Rebecca fell asleep before dessert. Should we wake her?"

"No, that's all right," Todd said, shaking his head. "She has to be exhausted by now." As he stood, he raised a hand to stop Olivia's movement. "Here, let us get those. You have to be exhausted, too."

Hannah stood next to him. "Yes, why don't you and Dad go in the living room and relax. We'll finish up in here." Strange, the thought of being in a room alone with Todd didn't make her feel uneasy the way it would have a few weeks before.

"Sounds good," he said. "Just let me go check on Rebecca, and I'll be in to help."

Her heart warmed as she watched his retreating form. He was such an amazing father. How could she ever have questioned whether he would be? She listened to the sound of his footsteps as he climbed the stairs and then stopped in the doorway of her childhood bedroom. Soon she heard footsteps on the stairs again.

"Boy, she's dead to the world," he said as he reentered the kitchen through the swinging door.

"I wonder why. It wasn't as if she woke up—and woke me up—at five-thirty or anything."

Todd stepped next to her until they were standing nearly shoulder-to-shoulder at the sink. Hannah rinsed the dishes and passed them to Todd to put in the dishwasher.

"Just five-thirty? I thought you said she got you up really early."

"It's early enough."

"So you still get grouchy when you miss your beauty sleep."

Hannah turned to give him her best evil eye, but Todd's silly grin made it impossible for her to hold the glower. "I guess some things never change."

"Some things do. I was glad to see Reverend Bob dating again. How long have he and Olivia been together?"

Hannah shrugged. "I don't know. Several months."

"You don't like her, do you?"

"I like her just fine."

His expression told her he didn't believe her. "But you don't think she's right for your dad."

Again, Hannah shrugged. "I don't know what I think."

"Would you think *any* woman was right for your dad?"

"Probably not."

"But you want him to be happy, don't you?"

Out of her side vision, she caught him watching her, waiting, expecting her to tell him what he already knew to be true. Reluctantly, she nodded. Of course, she wanted her father to be happy again. Maybe he would even be blessed to find someone with whom to share his life. She could still remember her father's devastation after her mother died. Todd was there. He remembered, too.

Todd poured the automatic detergent into the dishwasher and closed the door. "Olivia seems to make him happy."

"I know. I keep telling myself that. She's not all that bad really, even if I don't feel comfortable around her. She can't help it she's not—"

"Not your mother?"

"No, silly. Not Mary Nelson."

"Who? Your babysitter?"

"Mary's great, and I think she's been in love with Dad for years. He doesn't have a clue. Mary loves Rebecca, too." She paused, the memory of her child-care provider with her daughter bringing a smile to her lips. "She's the closest thing to a grandmother Rebecca's ever had."

"She has another grandma…and another grandpa," Todd said in a quiet voice.

"Sorry. I didn't mean—"

He waved away her apology. "Don't worry about it. My parents are dying to meet her." He shot her an embarrassed look. "Well, they're excited now that they've gotten over the shock of learning about her. They hope to visit in February."

"I'm sure Rebecca will love meeting them." For now, Hannah was just relieved that they'd changed the subject.

"You know you can't choose for your father, right?" Todd said, dragging them back to the old subject.

"I know."

A knock at the kitchen door ended the conversation. Reverend Bob stuck his head inside. "Oh, you are finished. We wondered what was taking you two so long."

Hannah shifted, worried her father had overheard, though she doubted he would have been smiling like that if he had. Grabbing the dishrag, she started wiping down the counter. "We were just finishing up."

Bob continued to stand holding the door open. He was wearing his long overcoat to cover his slacks and sports jacket.

"Olivia and I thought we'd take a stroll to work off our dinner. We would invite you two to join us, but we didn't expect that you'd want to wake Rebecca."

He probably wanted to be alone with his lady friend, too, but Hannah refrained from mentioning it.

"No, that's fine. We'll stay here," Todd told him.

"Why don't you two start a fire? Olivia and I will probably want to warm ourselves by it when we get back."

"Sure, we can do that."

With a wave, Bob backed out of the door.

Todd wiped his hands on a towel and crossed to the kitchen door. "I can't believe they would go out into that weather on purpose when they could stay inside and keep warm."

"Don't worry. You'll get used to the Michigan climate again. You did last time." She followed him down the hall to the family room where five stockings dangled from the mantel—three embroidered ones for Bob, Hannah and Rebecca, and two red felt socks, purchased just for this occasion.

He turned back to her. "The last time we were only moving here from Tennessee. This move has been much harder coming from a tropical climate."

"Maybe it's an age thing. You are a whole lot older this time."

"Speak for yourself, sweetheart. Isn't it great that we're the same age?"

She wrinkled her nose at him. "Well, anyway, we still need to build that fire. You know how to do it, right?"

"I was hoping you knew."

"Never a Boy Scout, eh? Well, allow me to demonstrate for you." Hannah crouched in front of the fireplace, opened the glass doors and twisted a black control just beneath the pile of logs. Golden flames leaped out and licked over the faux wood.

Todd broke out in a round of applause. "Okay, you got me. I didn't remember you having a gas fireplace."

"Dad had it put in a few years ago." She stood and warmed her hands near the fire before partially closing the doors.

Staring into the flame for several seconds, Todd approached the mantel and smoothed his index finger over the tiny Baby Jesus in the crystal crèche arranged on top.

"That belonged to my mother." Hannah stretched up to the mantel and ran her fingers over the sloping shape of one of the crystal Christmas trees that marked both ends of the display.

"I remember it. There are several things still in this house that remind me of her. She's been gone for seven years, and her fingerprints are still everywhere here."

Hannah's heart squeezed. It was just like Todd, the Todd she remembered, to reassure her that her mother's memory would be preserved. How had he known just how much she'd needed to hear that today when another woman's touches filled the kitchen and dining room?

"I wish you could have known her better."

"Yeah, me, too. She died about six months after we moved in."

"By the time you met her, the uterine cancer had already taken so much of her spirit." The flames drew Hannah's attention as she settled on the sofa and drew her stocking-clad feet up under her dress. "Sometimes it seems like so long ago that she died, and other times it feels like just yesterday."

"Yeah, I know what you mean."

His words drew her out of her haze. When she looked up at him, Todd's face was hidden in shadow.

"You know, I probably never would have survived those first few months, the first few years even, without you. So if I didn't remember to thank you then, I want to do it now. Thank you."

"You didn't need to thank me, then or now. I wanted to help if I could. You just didn't realize how strong you were. You would have found your way eventually on your own."

"Fortunately, we never had to know that for sure."

Todd watched Hannah closely as he tried to absorb what she'd just said. Her comment was as strange and unexpected as so many of the things she'd done lately, from including him in her private Christmas celebration to spending hours making that incredible photo album for him. What message was she trying to give to him?

"Have you ever wondered 'what if'?" The second the words were out of his mouth, Todd regretted speaking them. Why couldn't he just enjoy the moment? This was the first time since he'd moved back that Hannah had allowed him to get this close, and he had to sabotage it.

Todd rested his elbow against the mantel and waited. Instead of striking back as he expected she might, Hannah simply stared at him from across the room.

He rushed to backtrack. "I don't mean what if we hadn't made— Or if you didn't get—" Finally, he stopped himself, staring at the floor. "I don't know what I mean."

"Yes," she whispered.

His head jerked up, and he searched her face for whatever she wasn't saying.

Her eyes were shiny, and her tongue slipped out to moisten her lips. When Todd was convinced she wouldn't say more, she cleared her throat and began.

"I've wondered what if. About a lot of things."

"But not about having Rebecca." He didn't even need to pose it as a question. He knew what her answer would be.

She used the back of her hand to swipe at her eyes. "No. Never Rebecca. I've never even questioned my decision to keep her, though a lot of people thought I should have considered adoption."

Something cold gripped his insides. He'd always believed adoption to be a great thing—still did. Many strong families were built by the selflessness of birth mothers' difficult decisions.

But if Hannah had made that choice, he might never have known that their child existed. He wouldn't even have known to mourn the empty place in his life that would have been there without Rebecca.

The thought weighed so heavily on his mind that he crossed to the sofa where Hannah sat and slumped onto the opposite end.

Hannah turned so she faced him and leaned her back against the sofa's armrest. "I sometimes wonder what our lives would have been like if I'd told you as soon as I knew I was pregnant."

He'd wondered the same thing so many times himself and had blamed her for guaranteeing that neither of them would ever know. But now he couldn't work up the energy to continue holding a grudge.

"If only I'd told my father the whole story," Hannah continued, staring at her hands. "Dad would have convinced me to tell you." She lifted her head to meet his gaze. "You had the right to know."

"It's all in the past now." He leaned back and popped his feet on the box-shaped footstool next to the couch. "Anyway, I can't promise I would have come off as a hero back then. We both know I didn't make the best decisions at seventeen."

It was good to see her stark expression soften even though her eyes still looked damp.

"My decisions weren't exactly stellar, either."

Todd smiled, his memory of that teenage girl and the woman she had become melding. Her sweetness and vulnerability—things he'd loved about her but believed she'd lost—were still there, just buried beneath layers of self-protective armor.

"Whatever mistakes you made, you've done an amazing job with Rebecca. She's an incredible kid."

"She is pretty great, isn't she?" Hannah settled back into the sofa again, some of her tension from moments before seeming to ebb.

Todd found himself relaxing, too. "She's happy and kind and well-adjusted. You see, God always had a plan for her—for all of us."

Tilting her head, Hannah studied him, drawing her eyebrows together. "There it is again. You lived next to me for two years. You went to church every Sunday with your parents and even with me a few times. In all that time, I don't remember you talking about your faith."

"I didn't have much faith to speak of at the time," he said with a chuckle. "Oh, I believed in God and all. I'd heard the message from the cradle. It all seemed reasonable enough. I just didn't see any reason to take it as personally as you did."

Hannah suddenly straightened and lowered her feet to the floor. "Personally? If I'd been focused on my personal relationship with God, then— Oh, I don't know. But we weren't talking about me, were we? This was about you."

Todd shrugged. "The story of my faith journey is pretty pedestrian. Unoriginal. I had to hit rock bottom before I looked up."

Her front teeth pressed into her bottom lip, and for several seconds Hannah said nothing. But, in a whispered voice, as if she didn't want the answer but had to know, she finally asked, "When was that?"

"When I was ten thousand miles from here, on one of the most beautiful tropical islands in the world and so lonely that I thought I might die. It did no good to call. My letters just came back unopened. It felt as if someone had carved my heart out and left it beating outside my body."

Hannah squeezed her eyes shut and covered them with her hands. "Now that was graphic." When she lowered her hands, she crossed her arms over her chest in a nervous self-hug.

"Okay, it came from a teenager's point of view. One who'd been playing too many video games. But those were stark days. I'd been so stupid that I ended up losing everything that mattered. That's when I hit rock bottom."

"Then what happened?"

"I turned to God, and He came alive for me." Todd held his hands wide to show how obvious that answer was. "He was there, showing me that I wasn't alone. I didn't realize until later that He'd been there all along."

"I'm glad."

Todd drew his eyebrows together. "That I found faith?"

"That, too, but more than that." She paused to study her hands and push back the cuticles on two of her nails. But finally she looked back at him. "I'm glad you weren't alone. I know what that's like. To feel alone."

"Is that how you felt?"

She didn't answer right away, but her eyes looked shiny in the firelight and then a single tear traced down her cheek. "More than just alone, I felt abandoned. Even before I took the pregnancy test."

You abandoned me. She hadn't phrased it that way, but he felt the condemnation of it anyway. Closing his eyes, he could picture Hannah as she must have been then, sitting by herself in her room, keeping a terrifying secret locked up inside.

Of course, she felt abandoned, whether he'd intended it or not and despite that he'd had the argument of a lifetime with his father for taking the foreign assignment.

He couldn't change the fact that she'd been alone, perhaps even more alone than he'd felt without her.

"I'm so sorry I wasn't here."

"Yeah, me, too." She gazed into the fire for several seconds. "I'm sorry about a lot of things."

"Then we have something in common. I've been trying to apologize to you ever since I came back to town. Since before I even knew about Rebecca."

"There's no need for you to apologize."

"But could you do me a favor and let me anyway?"

At first she shrugged, but she finally nodded.

"I'm sorry about pressuring you into— Well, you know. A sexual relationship. You were only looking for comfort, just someone to talk to in those months after your mom died, and I read something more into it. I wasn't thinking about you, or consequences or sin. I thought only of myself."

Todd had always wondered how Hannah would react when he finally apologized, but her nervous laughter he definitely didn't expect.

"Pressure?" Hannah said when she finally stopped chuckling. "It wasn't like that, and you know it. You can try to take all the blame. For a long time, I would have been more than happy to let you.

"But it wasn't all your fault. I was there, too. We just became too close and got carried away."

"Thanks for saying that." Todd blew out a tired sigh. "We've caused each other so much pain. Do you think we can ever get past it?"

"We have to…for Rebecca's sake."

"What about for *our* sake, Hannah? Yours and mine?"

At first Hannah appeared confused. They hadn't spoken about anyone's needs but their daughter's since Todd had returned to town. It was probably a mistake to do it now, but Todd couldn't help himself.

"A long time ago you and I were friends. Good friends. We were good together."

Hannah started shaking her head. "It was a long time ago. Maybe we really can't go back."

"Can't? Why not?" Then he stopped himself. He couldn't push, or he might frighten her away. "We don't have to go back. But I would like to go forward. This is my what if. I think we owe it to ourselves to explore it."

"What are you saying?"

"I'm saying that I would be honored if you would consider going out to dinner with me one night this week."

"A date?"

The word seemed to clog her throat. Todd's throat tightened, as well. Had he asked too much too soon? Had he become too anxious to reach his ultimate destination and messed up the journey?

He would have backtracked again, perhaps even assured her that their date would only be as friends, if he hadn't heard the squeak of the front door from the other room.

"Hannah, Todd, we're back," Reverend Bob called out, as if he thought it necessary to announce himself.

Though they were adults and simply sitting on opposite ends of the couch, they both straightened and planted their feet on the floor. Sounds of the rustling of outerwear and then approaching footsteps followed.

Their moment, their sweet cocoon of time alone together, was ending, and Todd worried that his chance with Hannah was coming to a close along with it.

"Yes, a date. Well, what do you say?"

The wait for her answer seemed to take hours instead of seconds. She glanced at the doorway through which her father and Olivia would come in only seconds. Was she gauging the amount of time she had to put him off completely?

But then she turned back to him, her lips curving into the most beautiful smile in the world. "Yes, Todd, I'd love to have dinner with you."

Chapter Ten

"Are you sure this place isn't too expensive?" Hannah glanced around nervously, first at the crisp, white tablecloths and crystal stemware and then at the candles that cast the whole restaurant in a golden glow. At least he'd warned her the place would be dressy, or she might have worn jeans instead of the long, black-velvet skirt, cream sweater and the dress boots she'd chosen.

This place—maybe her accepting Todd's invitation altogether—might have been a mistake. He'd made reservations less than twenty-four hours after she'd agreed to have dinner with him, not even giving her time to change her mind.

"Well, I might be a little short. Do you think you can pick up the difference?"

Todd gave that mischievous half smile that had always made her feel light-headed and made her stomach tickle. "I can afford it. Maybe not every week, but I can afford it. I have a job now, remember?"

"But Five Lakes Grill? It's so extravagant." She

glanced out the restaurant's front window that faced Main Street. Garlands still wrapped the streetlamps and holiday lights still glimmered in the store across the street, but she could see a few signs in the windows that read After-Christmas Sale.

"You finally agreed to go out with me. I wanted to impress you. Did it work?"

Hannah glanced around the room again and then back at Todd. He'd impressed her, all right. Dressed all in black, from his wool sport coat to his turtleneck and trousers, he'd never looked more handsome. Even the candlelight seemed to give him special attention, dancing over the blond highlights that remained in his hair.

She cleared her throat. "You didn't have to impress me."

"But I did, didn't I?"

She nodded, pressing her hand over the flutter in her stomach. Though she glanced away from his intense gaze, she could still feel him watching her. Why was she so nervous, anyway? During the short span of their friendship, she'd gotten to know this man better than most people ever knew each other. They'd shared their deepest thoughts, their failures and their fears.

Todd had borne the pain of her mother's death as if the loss had been from his own heart. How could she have forgotten all those stolen hours of intimacy that had nothing to do with the physical and everything to do with why she'd fallen in love with him?

Then the idea struck her that although they'd shared food and conversation together so many times, they'd never gone on a real date before. Dating had seemed extraneous to the relationship they'd already built together.

"Can you believe this is our first date?"

Hannah stiffened at his words, and her cheeks warmed. She shouldn't have been surprised that his thoughts had traveled the same path as her own, but she was.

Either the candlelight hid her discomfort or he pretended not to notice, but he continued as if she'd already answered him.

"I don't know about you, but I'm really nervous."

An ironic chuckle bubbled inside her throat. "It doesn't seem right, does it?"

He shook his head. "We know each other too well for us to be nervous." His eyes took on a faraway look as he lifted a hard roll from the bread basket and buttered it. "Or at least we used to."

"We still do," she assured him, not because she didn't share his uncertainty but because she wanted so badly to erase that sadness from his eyes. She set a slice of nut bread on her bread plate but didn't take a bite.

"It's okay if we don't know every little thing about each other today," he said.

"What do you mean?" Unable to meet his gaze, Hannah looked down and traced spinning circles on the tablecloth with her fingernail.

"At one time, we knew each other better than anyone. We finished each other's sentences. Before I sneezed, you'd pass a tissue into my hand."

Her fingers calmed against the cloth as she allowed

the memories to blossom inside her thoughts where she'd once held them in perpetual winter. "It *was* like that with us, wasn't it?"

"I want it to be different this time."

As Hannah looked up from the table, Todd reached across it and covered her left hand with his right. How opposite their hands looked—hers finely boned and pale from the long Michigan fall and his hand, broad and strong, still clinging to its island tan. His skin felt so warm, his touch as sure as the man he'd grown to be.

It would be best for her to pull away discreetly—she knew that. Then both of them could pretend nothing had happened. But how could she pull away when the connection felt so right?

They stayed like that for a few minutes, just touching. Todd probably expected her to move her hand, but when she didn't, he finally spoke again.

"This is our first date. We've had many experiences together, but this is new. I want it all to be new like this."

Hannah gently removed her hand from his this time, and he lifted his fingers to let her go. Immediately, her skin felt cold.

"As nice as all this sounds, Todd, we can't rewrite history."

He nodded as if to concede that point. "But we can add new pages to our history. I know it—*we*—can be different together this time."

"Can there be a chance for us after all that's happened?" Even as she said it, she felt a wave of loss thinking that the past might need to remain the past and the future only an unattainable dream.

"Maybe this is a mistake. Maybe I shouldn't have agreed to come. If you want, we could leave instead of ordering. We're only ripping open old wounds and taking the chance that we'll create even deeper ones. Wounds that won't heal."

"We're doing all of that?" Todd held his finger to his lips as if in deep concentration. "I thought we were just having dinner."

Despite herself, Hannah laughed. Seconds before she'd been contemplating pain and loss, and now he had her laughing again.

Todd laughed with her, his deep baritone turning the heads of a few other restaurant patrons before he lowered his voice. "Now are you sure you're just a photo-taking accountant? I see a future for you on the stage. You have a flair for the dramatic."

"I like to keep my professional options open."

He smiled at first, but then his expression turned serious. "I know a lot has happened between us, but can't we think of tonight as just dinner? We can pretend we're just two single adults getting to know each other better. We'll keep all our baggage carefully hidden the same way everybody else does on first dates."

When Hannah paused for a moment to digest Todd's suggestion, the waiter must have seen the break in conversation as his chance because he approached the table to take their order. The parchment-style menu still rested on the table where she'd laid it earlier. She'd been too busy talking to even decide what she wanted to order.

She met Todd's gaze across the table. If she ordered, it would be admitting that she'd decided to stay after all. After a quick look at the menu selections, she turned back to the waiter and ordered a puree of butternut squash soup and roast duck in a bread pudding.

After Todd gave his order of potato-crusted Lake Superior whitefish and the waiter left the table, he turned back to Hannah, who was watching him.

"You sound as if you have a lot of experience in the first-date department." She shouldn't have brought it up again, but she couldn't help being curious.

Todd raised an eyebrow. "If a lot means the three times in the last five years that my mother insisted I attend this or that function with the daughter of some executive in Dad's company, then I'm a first-date expert."

"You are an expert compared to me," she said with a grin. "This is my *first* first date. I haven't had much interest in socializing with members of the opposite sex in the last few years."

"But you had a lot of offers, didn't you?" he said, though her comment appeared to surprise him.

Again, her cheeks felt warm, but she told him the truth, anyway. "Yes, I've had some offers."

"Especially from that one guy at your house. That Grant or somebody."

The way he avoided her gaze suggested that his memory of Grant Sumner wasn't as foggy as he would like her to believe. He wasn't immune to a little latent jealousy on the matter, either.

"Yes, Grant was one of them."

"What's the story with that guy, anyway?" he asked too casually.

"Grant's a great guy, a good friend, but he wasn't the right person for me." Hannah braced herself for Todd's knowing glance that would suggest he knew just who that right person was, but he only nodded. "I tried not to encourage him, but I guess he thought someday…"

Hannah took a deep breath, still wishing she'd handled the situation better. "Well, anyway, I wish he would come back to church. I've missed him lately."

"He's probably having a tough time letting you go. I know from experience how difficult that is."

She blinked. A jealous comment she would have expected, but Todd's compassion surprised her. Many things about this adult Todd surprised and pleased her. Still, the conversation had become too serious, so she decided to lighten the mood by adding, "A few others asked me out, too."

"You sure know how to kill a guy."

Hannah chewed her lip, trying not to smile. "The infant safety seat in the back of my car probably discouraged a few of them, but I still had some calls."

"I'm sure you did. Who could blame them?"

Soon they were both grinning, the discomfort that had been between them evaporating as their natural banter reemerged. They discovered that they did know each other, and what they didn't know about their current lives they began to learn.

They traded samples from their dinners as they joked about old times and shared stories from the more recent past. Often, the conversation would sneak back to their daughter's antics, and they laughed about those, as well.

Hannah felt more at peace than she'd been in a long time. She might have attributed it to the restaurant's ambience—the candlelight, the murmur of quiet voices, the sense of romance blossoming at nearby tables—but she decided not to lie to herself this time. Her feelings had nothing to do with the atmosphere and everything to do with the company.

She'd caught Todd watching her a few times when he'd thought she wouldn't notice. How could she not? The yearning in his gaze was strong enough to have awakened her from a sound sleep. Did Todd see a similar expression when she looked back at him?

No, she couldn't have thoughts like that—thoughts of any future beyond tonight. Not yet. Maybe not ever. The risk was too great. The prospect of another loss too terrifying. Would she ever be able to recover if she lost him again?

"What time did you tell Mary Nelson you would pick up Rebecca?" Todd asked, drawing her from the abyss of her dark thoughts. "I was surprised you took Rebecca there instead of having Mrs. Nelson come to your apartment."

Hannah set her fork aside and wiped her mouth with a napkin. "Oh, didn't I tell you? Rebecca gets to spend the night at Mrs. Nelson's. Mary insisted, and Rebecca was thrilled about sleeping in Mary's big guest bed."

"She'll really sleep there?"

"No, she'll be crawling into Mary's bed before the night is out. Mary doesn't mind."

"That's good news."

Hannah tilted her head to the side and gave him a quizzical look. "That Rebecca will be sneaking out of her bed in the middle of the night?"

Todd choked on the drink of water he'd just taken and coughed into his napkin before he could answer. "No. The good news is that you don't have to rush right home. We can have dessert and coffee."

"I don't know…" Hannah said, a smile pulling at her lips. Strange, as confused as she was about the two of them and what the future might hold, the one thing she did know for certain was that she wanted to stay right where she was. With him.

"Come on…tiramisu, chocolate mousse, sorbet…"

"Well, when you put it like that…"

Todd wiped his forehead with his napkin as if he'd just survived an ordeal. "Whew, you're a tough negotiator. I didn't think I'd make it through that one."

"I went easy on you that time."

"I appreciate that."

Hannah was rolling the last bite of the creamiest lemon tart she'd ever tasted around on her tongue when she caught Todd staring at her again. Her face felt warm under his regard, but she had to attribute at least part of the heat to the frothy cappuccino she'd been sipping.

Around them, the waitstaff had already begun clearing the tables and setting up for the next evening. Only one other couple remained at the corner table, probably newlyweds from the private glances they were exchanging.

"We should be getting home," Hannah told him.

"Why? Do you have a curfew? You said Rebecca was settled for the night."

Hannah wiped her mouth and set her napkin aside. "I have to work in the morning. Some of us don't have the week between Christmas and New Year's off each year. Some of us are just entering tax season where we'll barely be coming up for air until after April 15, and that's if we don't file a bunch of extensions."

"Oh, sorry. I forgot that you had to work." He studied his dessert plate for several seconds before his head popped up again. "But you could take just a few minutes longer…so I could walk you home, right?"

"Walk me home? Won't your car start?"

"It had better. It's only a month old. I just thought that it looks like the perfect night for a walk. It will be good for us, especially after that dinner."

Outside the restaurant's front window, dozens of snowflakes were skittering toward the ground, but trees planted in the Main Street sidewalk weren't swaying, so the wind from earlier in the day must have died down. She looked back at him.

"Then I'm glad you didn't pick a restaurant in Novi or Northville. I don't know if I would have been up for that hike."

"But you can handle the three blocks to your house, right?"

Hannah let her shoulders slump and tried to look exhausted. "Barely. But I'll make it."

She glanced out the window again. Huge, perfect snowflakes continued to twirl as if to a symphony of silence. The sky appeared clear and bright with the sliver of a moon towering above it all. Hannah was tempted to let herself believe that God had staged the whole setting just for the two of them, their own private glimpse of His amazing firmament.

It wasn't like her to give in to such romantic notions, but just this once, just in the expanse of time it took to reach her house, she wished for the freedom to be that young girl who still believed in happily ever after.

The wind picked up the minute they stepped outside, so Todd worried he might have made a tactical—and chilling—mistake. He tucked the scarf Hannah had given him more tightly around his neck and tugged his hat lower on his ears. Beside him, Hannah pulled the hood of her long dress coat up over her hair.

But the wind gust was only a long sigh before stillness resumed. He'd wanted a few more precious minutes with Hannah, and the car ride home would have been too short. He still had so much to say.

"I'm sorry this was our first date."

Hannah turned toward him, her face peering out from the hood's edge of faux fur. "What do you mean?"

"I should have taken you on dates when we were

younger. You deserved to be treated to nice dinners, movies and shopping trips. You deserved to be cherished." She had always deserved someone better than him, but he couldn't bring himself to say it aloud.

"We never needed anything like that. Everything between us was so simple. We were…just us."

"That's because I never had the guts to ask you on a real date. You had to settle for just watching TV or playing foosball in the basement."

"We had a great time."

"You deserved more."

They walked side by side in silence for a few seconds before Hannah started chuckling. "Even if you had asked me out, I'm not sure I would have been able to go. Dad and I never got around to the discussion of when I would be allowed to date. He always thought of me as his little girl."

The image of Rebecca immediately appeared in his mind. He could relate to Reverend Bob's feelings on that subject. He didn't even want to think about someday having to let some good-for-nothing teenage boy take his little girl out to the movies. That had to be the hardest thing for any father—to realize he was no longer the only love of his daughter's life.

Hannah continued as though unaware of how many years forward Todd's thoughts had traveled.

"When I wouldn't give the name of my baby's father, I thought I was keeping this huge secret," she said with a chuckle. "It wasn't as if I had tons of opportunities to sneak out with boys. Not everyone would have known immediately, but for those close to me, their list of possible candidates was short."

"I'm probably the only one who thought it could have been someone else."

Hannah lifted a shoulder and let it drop, but she didn't say anything.

"I'm sorry I jumped to the conclusion that anyone else could have been Rebecca's father. All I had to do was look at her to know the truth. And I should have known you wouldn't—" Todd cleared his throat. This subject matter was nothing if not delicate. "That was just my stupid jealousy talking."

"There never could have been anyone but—"

Though Hannah stopped herself, Todd realized what she'd almost said: *you.* She'd already told him she hadn't dated in all these years, but was she really saying there was no one else for her? Just as he'd always known that Hannah was the only woman for him?

Before he could stop himself, Todd reached over and closed his gloved hand protectively over Hannah's. He felt that same wave of wonder, of rightness that he'd experienced when he'd touched her hand in the restaurant. The sense was so powerful that he wondered if she could feel it, too.

But insecurities immediately invaded his peace. Would she pull away as she had earlier? Maybe she'd only been talking about her intention to avoid sexual temptation until she was married, and she hadn't been indicating anything about her feelings for him.

He waited, his heart pounding, his palm damp under

the glove. He didn't even realize that they'd stopped walking until Hannah looked up at him and then down at their joined hands. Instead of pulling away, she shifted her hand until their gloved fingers laced.

Neither said a word. Neither had to. With her simple movement, like a tacit agreement made with touch, everything changed. They had so many possibilities, when not long ago there had been so few.

With the wider-spaced streetlamps to guide them and the occasional passing vehicle and the crunch of snow beneath their feet as the only sounds, they continued up Commerce Road, turning left on Union Street to reach Hannah's apartment.

The wind picked up again, but Todd barely felt the chill. Hannah was this warm presence beside him, her hand fitting comfortably in his. The delicate, floral scent of her hair drifted into his nostrils, and he wanted nothing but to inhale the sweetness.

At her front steps, they paused, their hands unlacing and falling back to their sides. The temptation to draw Hannah into his arms was so overwhelming that Todd shoved his hands into his pockets to prevent it.

Hannah turned toward him, her face peeking out from the furry hood, but she stared at the ground and chewed her lip. He could just imagine what she had to be thinking. Did she dread the moment he would kiss her, or did she worry he wouldn't want to? The irony tempted him to smile. He couldn't imagine a time when he would be near Hannah and not want to kiss her, to hold her, to claim her as his own.

But now wasn't the time for any of those things. This moment was too important. He had too much to show her.

Finally, Hannah glanced up at him. "Thank you for dinner. I had a really nice time."

"Me, too."

"Well, I had better…" She let her words trail off, her gaze darting to her front door.

Todd jutted out his right hand and waited.

Hannah drew her eyebrows together and tilted her head to the side.

He only smiled, lowering his hand. "In case you're worried, I don't plan to kiss you tonight."

"I wasn't worried," she said, though everything about her tight demeanor suggested she was—either pro or con.

"Now don't get me wrong. I'm not opposed to the idea."

An embarrassed grin settled on her lovely mouth. "I'm not sure I understand."

"This is a first date. I wouldn't want to offend you by kissing you on our first date, so…" Again, he extended his hand, and she accepted it. The gesture felt surprisingly intimate because of the promise inherent in it. He would show her more respect this time. He would treat her the way she deserved to be treated.

Clearing her throat, Hannah stepped to the door and unlocked it. "Thanks again. I'm glad we did this."

"Me, too." He had descended the porch steps when he stopped and spoke over his shoulder. "You see, Hannah, everything will be different this time."

Chapter Eleven

Different. Todd had warned Hannah to expect that, but he hadn't prepared her for just how wonderful spending time with him would be. He'd proven both of those things so many times in the past three days as she'd seen almost as much of him as when he'd lived next door. Who could blame her for enjoying every minute of it?

Even as Hannah's fingers clicked across the keys of her office computer late Friday morning, she could still picture Rebecca's smiling face and hear her laughter as they'd taken her skating for the first time on the tiny ice rink at Central Park.

She touched her left hand with her right, remembering how nice it had been to hold hands with Todd on the couch after they'd put their daughter to bed. She needed to concentrate on the figures on the screen in front of her, but it was too tempting to remember the funny things he'd said and the way he looked at her that warmed her all the way to her heart.

"What are you smiling about? I thought you said those year-end figures were a mess."

Hannah jerked her head to see her boss, Harold Lasbury, standing in her office doorway looking at her with one of those strange expressions he reserved for anyone who wasted too much time laughing or smiling. Her cheeks burned.

"Oh, they were, but I'm finally whipping them into shape. I've already reconciled the bank statement and have posted the cash disbursements and cash receipts."

He cleared his throat. "Well, that's good. You'll want to compute the annual depreciation of equipment after lunch."

Hannah nodded, though she already knew well what was necessary to finish the client's year-end accounting. Sometimes Harold seemed to forget that she already had an accounting degree.

He started to leave but stopped and turned back to her. "Oh, you have a…guest in the waiting area."

Guest? She'd never heard her boss refer to a client that way before, and she certainly hadn't scheduled any client appointments the last workday before the new year. That her boss raised an eyebrow before continuing to his own office only confused her more.

Tightening the hair clip at her nape and straightening her suit jacket, Hannah headed to the waiting area, preparing herself mentally to welcome an additional client on a day when she was too busy to even take a lunch hour.

But the sight that greeted her when she reached the

cramped room, with standard-issue waiting chairs and salmon-colored wallpaper, made her smile again. Todd sat in one of the cushioned seats, a picnic basket taking up most of the seat next to him.

"What are you doing here?" she asked. "I told you I couldn't have lunch today." She wondered if it was okay for her to be secretly pleased about a visit that would put her behind for the rest of the afternoon.

He indicated the basket next to him. "No, you said you couldn't *leave* for lunch today. I just wanted to make sure you wouldn't go hungry."

"Thanks."

He stood and grabbed the basket handle. "Let's go in your office and eat so you can get back to work."

"What do you have in there?"

"Only the best impromptu picnic fare that money can buy." He followed her into her office and set the basket on her desk. "Sandwiches from Village Deli with cherry turnovers for dessert from Milford Baking Company."

"Boy, you had to work to get this stuff. Crossing Main Street at the lunch hour is like taking your life in your own hands."

"I do think some of the drivers believe those pedestrian crosswalks in the middle of the street are just suggestions." Todd set three sandwiches and two cans of soda on the desk and then pulled out a white bakery bag.

"Are all three of those for me?"

"You always did have an appetite twice the size of that tiny frame of yours." He paused, chuckling. "But I was hoping to eat at least one of the sandwiches."

In the end, they each ate a turkey sandwich and tore the ham down the center. Together, they demolished the pastries until there were only flaky crumbs.

Hannah licked a drop of tart cherry filling off her thumb and wiped it with her napkin. "I guess I was hungrier than I thought. Thanks for doing this."

"An early New Year's present. So how come you're working so hard when the rest of the world is kicking back for the holiday?"

"We have the year-end accounting to do for several of our corporate clients. That means year-end corporate tax returns and year-end payroll. We have to analyze and post the cash disbursements, which means figuring out which accounts they belong in. Then we have to go through the cash receipts, making sure they're all for sales. After that, we compute annual depreciation of equipment and do comparative analysis with figures from prior years."

"So in other words you're just sitting around waiting to ring in the New Year."

Hannah raised her hands in a mock surrender. "Oh no. You caught me."

"Well, I don't want to keep you from your afternoon nap, so..." He was grinning as he cleared away the empty wrappers, shoving them back into the basket. "We sure can put the food away. We don't need to wonder where Rebecca got her healthy appetite from."

"Or her strange sense of humor."

"Or her beauty."

"Are you complimenting yourself there?" she asked, though she felt warm inside.

"One of her parents, anyway."

Instead of waiting for her to find some clever retort, Todd took his basket and headed toward the door. "I'll call you tonight, okay?"

"Okay."

Todd had called three nights in a row, and she found she could get used to the regularity of it. She could get used to a lot of things about the last few days, but she didn't allow herself to dwell on them.

"Thanks again for doing this."

"Anytime."

With a wave, he was gone. Hannah couldn't help feeling the acuteness of his absence. It was as if all the laughter in the room had left with him.

Yes, they were different together this time but not in the way Todd must have meant with his promise. He'd always treated her as if she were someone precious to him. That hadn't changed with time or distance. But they were different people now. They'd made mistakes and had learned to live with their consequences. They'd wounded and been wounded. Yet somehow they'd found a way to continue on despite their scars.

Hannah stared at her computer screen, but she kept imagining Todd's image in the pattern of numbers— as the boy he'd once been and as the man he'd become.

She'd loved that boy; she could finally admit that to herself. Did she feel the same thing for him now that he'd emerged from the milieu of youth as this amazing, strong man? She shook her head, the incongruity so clear in her thoughts. If this scary, thrilling feeling was love, then it wasn't the same at all. It was stronger. Deeper. Emotional and spiritual in a way that only came with maturity.

She was so tempted to give in to the feeling, to let it soothe and heal. But she had to think this time. More than just two hearts were involved now. She had Rebecca to consider.

And even if she were certain that this was the best thing for all of them, would love be enough to make her forgive and forget, or would the seeds of distrust hidden just below the surface still linger? Would she ever be able to trust Todd fully with her heart?

The sounds of someone clearing his throat brought Hannah back from her dark thoughts. Harold stood in her office doorway with his arms crossed over his rounded chest. Hannah straightened in her seat. It was the second time her boss had caught her daydreaming in one day. She really was trying to begin the New Year in the unemployment line.

"Staring at the computer screen is not going to get those forms completed by five o'clock."

Hannah shook her head to expel the last of the errant thoughts. "I'm sorry, Harold. I just need to get focused."

"Too much picnic food?"

"No, it's not that."

"Big New Year's plans distracting you?"

Well, there was a certain church service that was taking on an extra significance this year, but that wasn't her current distraction, so she shook her head.

"Then I trust you'll expend the extra effort to ensure that our paying clients have their year-end reports completed correctly?"

"Yes, sir."

Her ringing desk phone saved Hannah from any parting comment from her boss. "Harold Lasbury and Associates. How may I help you?"

"Is this Hannah Woods?"

She started. Callers didn't usually ask for her first but more often were transferred to her when she had been assigned their year-end reports or 1040s. "This is she."

"This is David Littleton."

"Oh. Deacon Littleton, what can I do for you? I can schedule your appointment for filing your personal tax return, but I don't have any available until mid-January."

He cleared his throat. "Um…no…this is another matter."

An unsettling feeling crowded Hannah's insides. Deacon Littleton was always direct, not one to mince words in order to protect feelings.

"Is something wrong?"

"Oh, probably not. I've probably just made one of those bookkeeping mistakes we volunteers do on occasion, and I was wondering if you might take a peek at the church books for me."

"Well, today I am really swamped, but—"

"Oh, there's no real rush." He paused as if considering. "In fact, don't worry about it. I'm sure I can find the mistakes."

"You're sure? I don't mind looking over them at all. I even have a day off Monday since New Year's is on Sunday."

"No. That's all right. Enjoy your day off. If I can't find them, I'll be sure to ask for help."

"You do that, okay?"

"You're the professional."

Hannah ended the call, feeling relieved that she didn't have to add another task to her growing to-do list. But something about the call still didn't sit right with her. Why had the deacon asked for her help if he was only going to retract his request?

Another thing, Deacon Littleton had been keeping the church's books for as long as Hannah could remember, and the paperwork he kept was impeccable. He never made mistakes. What was different this year? And what had the deacon so worried?

Hannah shook away the uncomfortable thoughts and focused on the form on the screen. If she had the choice, she would just give up and call the day a wash. First, questions about Todd and now concerns about church.

The owners of Village Gifts and Milford Beauty Supply had the right to expect her total attention on their business accounting. Maybe her boss had the right idea. Harold loved crunching numbers to the exclusion of everything else. She needed to follow his example, at least during office hours. She would have to figure out her love life and the puzzle at church on her own time.

* * *

"Daddy, why are you and Mommy not married?"

Todd jerked, an unfortunate reflex given he was sitting cross-legged on the floor, balancing a wiggly Rebecca, a messy-haired Miss Gabrielle and a copy of *Alice's Adventures in Wonderland* in his lap. The child's backside, the doll and the book's hard cover hit the floor before Alice could even attend the Mad Hatter's Tea Party.

"Oh. Sorry, kiddo," he said, pretending not to notice the other adults in the children's department at the nearly new Milford Public Library. They'd heard the question as clearly as he had and were trying not to get caught staring.

"Ouch, Daddy. That hurt." Rebecca frowned at him, rubbing the offended part of her before climbing back into his lap. All trespasses forgiven, she situated Miss Gabrielle, which was discreetly covered in her dress that day, and collected poor *Alice,* returning it to her father's hands.

But instead of opening the book and continuing reading Lewis Carroll's classic story, Todd set it aside. How could he explain something so complicated to a four-year-old? He was tempted to distract her, to offer to find more books or to go eat ice cream, but Rebecca deserved better than that. She deserved a straight answer given at a level she would understand. It was his turn to answer their daughter's questions. Hannah had been answering them for a long time.

"How about we find a different place to sit so we're

not on the floor?" They didn't need an audience for this conversation, either, but he didn't mention that.

Taking her hand, Todd led her into one of the tiny glass conference rooms and shut the door behind them. Setting the book they'd been reading on the table, he sat in one of the chairs. Instead of sitting in the other, Rebecca scrambled up into his lap.

"Why did we go in the room?"

"You asked me a question, and I wanted to answer it."

She seemed to consider and then nodded. "Okay."

"I wish your mom and I had been married when we were younger." He brushed his hand over her tiny blond pigtails. "Before we had you."

"Why didn't you?"

"Because we made too many mistakes. And then I lived too far away. I didn't know you lived here." He couldn't see any reason beyond payback to tell Rebecca he hadn't known she existed, so he kept that knowledge to himself.

"You don't live far away now."

"No, I don't." Todd couldn't help smiling. His little girl just might have a future in law given the way she could already argue her case.

Rebecca lay back in his lap until her head hung upside down over the side of the chair with her pigtails drooping toward the floor. "Daddy, are you and Mommy still mad at each other?"

The question surprised him, but it shouldn't have. Did he really think that Rebecca, who rarely missed anything, would have been oblivious to the tension that had been stretched tight between Hannah and him in the beginning and the gradual loosening of the rope?

"No, honey, I don't think we are."

Her head popped up, and she scrambled down from his lap.

"Then you can get married."

"You see, it's not that simple." But even as he said it, he wished it could be.

"Then we could all live in the same house, and you wouldn't have to live in your apartment, and we could get a dog."

"A dog?" Todd threw his head back and laughed. "That's what all of this is about? A dog?"

Rebecca slumped in the chair next to his and crossed her arms. "At Max's house, they got a puppy for Christmas. His name is Rudy. Max's mommy got married last year…" She let her words trail off to signify that she'd made her point: marriage first, then dog.

"Honey, even if your mother and I did get married, that doesn't mean we could get a dog." When those eyes started to fill, he considered telling her that even kids who lived with one parent sometimes had dogs. Still, realizing that a comment like that might make Hannah angry enough to remain a single parent indefinitely, he kept that bit of trivia to himself.

"But I *want* a dog."

A giant tear rolled down her cheek until Todd reached over and brushed it away. After a few more followed it, he pulled her from the other chair back into his lap.

Was this really about a dog or about other things in her life that were just as out of her control? If only he knew. This feeling of helplessness was a part of the parenting experience. Hannah had explained that much to him. Would he always feel the need to hang the moon for his little girl and be frustrated when he couldn't?

Well, he would never be able to guarantee that life was perfect for Rebecca, but the one thing he could do for her was to love her mother. He was becoming really good at it. And if he had anything to say about it at all, he would make sure that Rebecca's parents were married, and they were all living together—with or without a dog—by next Christmas.

Chapter Twelve

The scents of pine and melting wax wafted through the darkened church sanctuary as candlelight cast the bowed heads in shadow. Todd realized he should have been praying, too, spending some time in quiet meditation as a brand-new year approached, but he couldn't keep his eyes closed while the woman he loved sat next to him, already an answer to his prayers.

In the candlelight, Hannah looked so beautiful and serene as a strand of her hair that she'd worn loose fell forward over her cheek. It looked like spun gold, and he knew if he brushed the hair back from her face, it would feel like it, too.

He shook his head. He shouldn't be thinking thoughts like these, especially here in church. But then where could he go that he wouldn't think of Hannah? She lived with him at home, at work, in his dreams, even in his prayers. He had to tell her that, to make her understand that they were meant for each other.

Nervous tension flooded his system, making him

shift in his seat. What if after all the time they'd spent with each other, she didn't agree that they should be together? Still, his need to connect with her was stronger than his misgivings, so he closed his hand over hers.

Without opening her eyes, she leaned toward him. "You're supposed to be praying in the new year," she whispered.

"I pray better this way."

He laced their fingers, resting their hands on the pew between them. It felt like such a significant statement to hold hands with her in church—like an announcement of their connection before the whole Hickory Ridge community. Already they'd stood sharing a hymnal, which he'd always considered a statement in itself.

Because he expected her to pull away, to be uncomfortable with the message they telegraphed to the rest of the congregation even in the low lights, his heart warmed as her long, elegant fingers pressed into the back of his hand. It made what he intended to say later tonight seem even more right.

"Amen," Reverend Bob said into the sound system on the lectern, ending the period of quiet meditation. "Now that we've prepared our hearts and minds, please file forward to accept Communion in silence."

Todd leaned close to Hannah. "Do you think Rebecca's asleep by now?"

"Mary promised she would put her to bed by ten."

"It was nice of her to take Rebecca overnight again so we could attend the service."

"She's like that." She glanced up at her father and back at Todd. "Now hush, will you?"

After the solemn service and Andrew Westin's inspiring closing prayer, the holiday event ended just after the stroke of midnight. Church members filed silently out of the dark sanctuary into the lighted vestibule before sharing cheer and good wishes to celebrate the arrival of the new year.

While the church building emptied, Todd retrieved both of their coats from the rack. A gray-haired man approached them, already wearing his coat.

"Todd, have you met David Littleton?" When he shook his head, Hannah turned to the other man. "Deacon Littleton, this is Todd McBride."

The two men shook hands, but the older man kept his gaze focused on Hannah. "I'll let you know about that other thing, okay?"

"Call any time if you need help. I mean it."

Deacon Littleton nodded and continued past her.

"What was that all about?"

"Oh, tax season begins. The questions come from everywhere." But she continued to watch the older man as he left, a perplexed expression on her face.

When Hannah reached for her coat, Todd rested a hand on her arm to delay her. "Can we go somewhere? I'd like to talk to you about some things."

Her eyes widened, and she glanced through the glass doors into the night. "You want to go somewhere in that? It's New Year's. It's probably crazy out there."

As if to punctuate her comment, the multiple pops

of firecrackers being set off in a nearby neighborhood drifted in as someone opened the church door. Somewhere in the distance, someone shot a rifle into the air.

Standing next to them in his Michigan State Police jacket, Brett Lancaster grumbled. "Let the 9-1-1 calls begin. When will people ever realize that firearms, illegal fireworks and holiday celebrations don't mix?"

His wife, Tricia, came up beside him. "Don't mind him. I just have to go home and relieve the sitter, but he has to go into work tonight."

"Sorry to hear that, Brett." Todd patted his shoulder. "Stay safe on patrol, okay?"

"Better pray that the rest of the drivers on the road will stay sober and safe."

"I'll pray for that, buddy."

Todd was relieved when the other couple continued past them to shake hands with Reverend Bob and Andrew. Making polite conversation was difficult when he was anxious to get Hannah alone and say things that needed to be said.

Turning to Hannah, he gestured toward the sanctuary, still illuminated only by candlelight.

"You want to talk in *there?*" she asked.

She chewed her bottom lip in the nervous way he'd come to recognize. If she was flustered at the prospect of a serious conversation with him, he could just imagine how she would act if she knew what he was going to say. He did know, and he was nervous enough for the both of them.

"I doubt we'll get in trouble for talking in there since the service is over."

"I didn't mean—" She rolled her eyes yet seemed to relax a little. "Okay."

He led her past several stained glass windows with candles in their sills and past the candelabras near the rounded stage platform and the altar. In the front pew, opposite the organ, he sat and motioned for Hannah to join him.

Her gaze darted toward the lighted vestibule. "Dad will want to lock up soon."

"Hannah, don't worry. There are still a few people out there. And even if there weren't, Reverend Bob would give us a few minutes to talk." He patted the seat next to him. "Please sit."

With a sigh, she lowered herself into the seat. "You sure are persistent."

"You bring that out in me."

Hannah wore a small smile, but she focused on her wringing hands. "I'm sorry about that."

"You bring out all kinds of feelings in me."

Her hands stilled, and slowly she looked up at him, her eyes searching for answers.

He didn't know how to phrase it, where to start, but he couldn't keep it bottled up any longer, either. "You know how much you matter to me, don't you, Hannah? You understand that I returned with this grand scheme to win you back."

He didn't even pose the last as a question. If she'd been watching or listening to anything he'd done or said in the last few weeks, she had to know. "And then you told me about Rebecca."

Hannah lowered her gaze to her hands. "We don't have to do this. Rehashing it isn't going to change history."

"I'm not talking about history." He paused, the sound of his heartbeat so loud that she had to hear it. "I'm talking about the future."

"Future?" Her head lifted slowly.

He couldn't decipher her tight expression, but he couldn't stop now. She needed to know how he felt. He desperately needed her to know. What she did with that knowledge was up to her.

"I told you once that I loved you, and then I promptly disappeared from your life."

"Todd, what you are trying to say?"

"Oh, right. I said I wasn't going to talk about the past." He paused long enough to take her hands. "This isn't *in* the past. I care so much about you. I always have. And I'm not going anywhere this time."

Slowly, he returned her hands to her lap.

"I just wanted you to know that."

"That's it?"

Hannah looked as shocked as he was that she'd spoken those particular words.

"What were you expecting? A proposal?" He couldn't help it. A chuckle bubbled up in his throat, deflating the air of romance he'd hoped to build with all that candlelight.

"Yes. No. I don't know." She turned and covered her face with her hands, but pretty soon she chuckled, too.

It felt so surreal, the two of them sitting shoulder to shoulder with Hannah in the front pew of the darkened room, laughing until their eyes grew damp. But then he and Hannah had never been about candles, flowers or greeting cards with someone else's flowery words on them. They'd always written their own poetry of simplicity, a natural accord that couldn't be squeezed into a box of chocolates.

Laughter was intrinsic to the time they'd spent together, years ago and today, so it was only right that it would echo off the walls at a moment like this. Still, the melodic sound in her throat stopped the moment he slipped his arm around her shoulders.

"Now don't misunderstand me. I have every intention of asking you to marry me someday soon, when the time is right. We belong together…as a family." He tried not to notice how her shoulders tightened slightly under his touch.

"You can think of this as fair warning. I'd like to think of it as my commitment for the new year." He held his breath, waiting for the answer that could bolster his hope for the future or dash it before they'd really even tried.

"Don't you worry…that it's too late for us?"

The catch in her throat startled him as much as what she'd said. She hadn't begged him to propose today and be done with it, but she hadn't told him to forget asking, either. It was something.

When he turned to face her, he saw something more. Tears glistened in her eyes, and one traced down her cheek. The tears were his undoing. With his thumb, he wiped her cheek, and then he cradled her face in his hands.

"No, it's not too late. It can't be."

Two more tears escaped her stronghold, but she didn't answer. Maybe she couldn't. As Todd brushed the tears away with his thumbs, he couldn't help reaching slightly farther to feather a touch across her lips. They were just as smooth as he remembered. Just as perfect.

"I would really like to kiss you right now, but I want it to be your decision, too. May I kiss you, Hannah?"

For several heartbeats, she said nothing, did nothing. Dread clawed at the edges of his consciousness. Would now be when she told him that it would never work between them? Would he have to continue facing her every week while he planned outings with their daughter, knowing she would never be his?

She nodded, and his whole world shifted.

With utmost gentleness, he drew her to him and pressed his lips to hers. He remembered this—the softness of her lips, their sweet taste—but his memories paled in comparison to this moment. Kissing her here in church felt like a promise before God, a preview of the day, if she allowed him to, he would finally make her his wife.

Todd lowered his hands to her shoulders and touched his lips to hers a second time, just a brief caress but one with which he offered his heart as a gift. "Happy New Year, Hannah."

"Happy New Year."

And it would be a happy one. He just knew it.

The flash of the overhead lights coming on in the sanctuary caused the two of them to jump apart. Reverend Bob stood just inside the door, his hand on the switch.

"Oh, you two are in here?" the minister asked too innocently.

"Yeah, Dad, but we were just leaving."

"Oh, no hurry. I just need to put out those candles before I lock up."

Todd popped up from his seat. "Here, we'll help with those." He climbed the steps to the platform and lifted the brass snuffer to extinguish the flames in the candelabra.

"Yeah, we can help," Hannah said as she stood.

"Thanks, you two, but Hannah, it would help me more if you could go out to the Family Life Center and check the locks on the rear doors."

She shot a nervous look at Todd, but she nodded and ascended the side aisle to the exit.

Todd didn't waste any time waiting for the minister to approach him. He crossed to the row of stained glass windows where Reverend Bob was working.

"I take it you'd like to talk to me."

"You'd be right." Bob turned to him and met his gaze directly.

"I have an idea what you saw, but I can explain."

"Do you have something you feel guilty about?"

Todd shook his head. "No, sir, I don't."

"Good. I'm glad."

"You have to know that I love your daughter." He waited for the minister's nod before he continued. "I came here planning to win her back—even before I knew about our child."

Bob extinguished another candle before he turned to him. "What are your plans now?"

"My intentions? They're honorable, I assure you. I'd rather die than hurt her or Rebecca."

"You've done it before."

"I never will again."

"See that you don't."

"See that he doesn't do what?" Hannah called out from the door at the rear of the room.

Both men turned to look at her guiltily, but neither answered.

"All right then," she said, wearing a frown that said it was anything but all right. "If you two are finished discussing me behind my back, I'm ready to leave now."

Todd moved up the aisle toward her. "Don't get mad, Hannah. Your dad's just concerned about you."

Still, she turned away from him to focus her frown on her father instead. The minister shrugged, unrepentant.

"I'm not a child anymore, Dad."

"You'll always be my little girl," he said simply.

"You think he's bad. Your dad's a pushover compared

to what I'm going to be like the first time some teen-age boy asks Rebecca out. I'll put a little fear in him."

Bob chuckled. "I feel sorry for that young man."

"Me, too," Hannah agreed. Her expression had finally softened. "Rebecca and I don't need any pity, though. I think we both have pretty great dads."

Twenty minutes later, Hannah stood on her front porch with Todd, nervousness and anticipation combining with the brand-new January chill. Would he kiss her again? She hoped so. She'd never felt so safe as she had tonight in his arms. If only she'd been brave enough to tell him the feelings in her heart. But, as always, she'd been a coward.

"This was the best New Year's I've ever had," Todd said as he shifted his position so he could block the wind from reaching her.

The gallant gesture made her smile. Not so long ago, when he was fresh from balmy Singapore, Todd would have been suggesting that they both go inside, out of the wind.

"I agree. It was the best."

"It's going to be an even better year for us." He drew her into his arms, holding her tightly against his thick coat.

As she rested her head against his shoulder, Hannah closed her eyes and breathed in his musky cologne. It felt so right that it should have frightened her, but for once she just let herself enjoy the wonder of being with him.

After a few seconds or minutes, Todd drew away

from her and rested his hands on her shoulders. "I love you, Hannah. I've wanted to tell you that for so long."

Hannah's chest squeezed, and her eyes burned. Until that moment, she didn't realize how much she'd longed to hear him say those words, as well. It wasn't the first time he'd spoken them, but this time meant so much more.

He smiled at her and traced his gloved thumb along her jawline. Placing his fingers beneath her chin, he lifted her mouth toward his, but he paused as if again asking her permission. She nodded and closed her eyes, waiting.

His kiss was soft and unhurried. Hannah had never felt so cherished as she did at that moment in the shelter of his arms. When he finally pulled away, he squeezed his eyes shut and leaned his forehead against hers.

"Why do all my purest intentions flee the moment you're in my arms?" he said with a chuckle. "Sorry."

"Why are you sorry? You only kissed me."

He took a deep breath and shook his head as he took a step back from her. "I can't ever imagine kissing you and not wishing for more."

Hannah stared at the ground. Even in the wind, her cheeks felt warm. But somehow his confession made her feel more treasured. "I guess I shouldn't invite you in then."

"Probably not a good idea." He smiled. "I want to do this right this time. I can wait."

They stood there in silence as the chill seeped

through their outerwear. Hannah tightened her jaw to keep her teeth from chattering.

"You know, I loved you even then," he said quietly, drawing her attention back to his face. "Even when I wasn't mature enough to know what to do with all those feelings."

"I knew, even then." The time had come; she could feel it. Could she finally confess aloud what had been in her heart all along? Clearing her throat, she whispered, "I love you, too. Then and now."

Hannah waited, expecting the panic inspired by the words to settle in, heavy and immovable. Instead, her heart felt light, as if a weight she hadn't even known was there had been lifted.

On a sharp intake of air, Todd drew her into his arms again, cradling her head against his shoulder. "I've waited so long to hear you say that. I thought you would never forgive me. I thought—"

He stopped himself, but Hannah heard the thick emotion in his voice. "You do forgive me, don't you?"

"Of course, I do," she heard herself assuring him. And she had, really. She couldn't continue to hold him accountable for leaving her when it wasn't his decision. Todd so clearly trusted her with his heart. Maybe one day she could learn to trust that way, too. Completely. For now, loving him would have to be enough because it was all she had to give.

Chapter Thirteen

"Happy New Year!"

"Happy New Year to you, too, Mom." Todd pressed the portable phone to his ear and peeled open his eyes one by one. The only light filtering into the room came from a streetlamp outside his apartment, and his bedside clock read six forty-five.

"You didn't happen to check the time before you called, did you?"

"Of course," Sharon McBride said. "It's nearly eight. I just cleaned up the dinner dishes. We had pot roast with red-skin potatoes."

"Sounds delicious," he said, though he doubted he could have eaten even that at this hour. "There's a thirteen-hour time difference, remember?"

"I never can remember how many hours it is." Her chuckle filtered through the phone line along with some intercontinental static. "But you need to get up for church soon, anyway."

He could have slept two hours longer, and he'd been

too keyed up to close his eyes before three o'clock that morning, but he kept that information to himself. Flipping the light on, he climbed out of bed and padded into the kitchen. He wouldn't be able to go back to sleep after this conversation anyway.

Sharon cleared her throat audibly. "Todd William McBride, are you going to tell me or not?"

"Tell you what?" Todd couldn't help smiling because he knew exactly *what*. Finally he took pity on her. "No, I didn't propose to Hannah yet."

"Why not?"

"It was too soon."

When she didn't say anything Todd knew from experience that his mother expected him to explain. "I don't know. I'd even bought the ring and had it with me, but I felt like God was telling me to wait."

"Can't argue with that." Though her tone made it sound as if she wished she could. "You did send Hannah our love, didn't you?"

"Yes, I did. Don't worry, Mom. I'm going to ask her." He poured himself a bowl of cereal and opened the refrigerator for the milk.

"Well, don't wait too long. Your dad and I are looking forward to coming back for the wedding. And I can't wait to get my hands on my grandbaby."

"Remember, Mom, Rebecca's not a baby anymore."

"Then you'd better marry her mother and give her your name before my granddaughter is a teenager who doesn't want to be spoiled by her Nana McBride."

It was such a relief to hear his mother talk that way,

showing that she was ready to accept her grandchild with open arms.

"Rebecca will let you spoil her even before we get married. She's very generous that way."

"I'm sure she is." She chuckled for a few seconds and then became serious again. "Still, don't you think it's time for you to bring your family together? Past time?"

Todd nodded though she couldn't see him. "That's what I plan to do, and it's going to be perfect."

"Remember, honey, perfect is an awful lot to expect from anyone. We're imperfect people. We're just loved by a perfect God."

"She forgave me, Mom. For leaving her behind. For…everything."

"That's wonderful, honey. Now don't you think it's time you forgave yourself?"

His mother ended the conversation soon after, but her question followed him while he finished breakfast and showered for church. Why had it been so easy to forgive Hannah, even for keeping Rebecca from him, when it was so hard to forgive himself for the sins of his past?

What if God was so selective with His forgiveness? Todd shook his head over the ludicrous idea. God always forgave, and Todd knew he'd been forgiven from the moment he'd first repented his sin with Hannah. And yet he couldn't let it go. Even when he'd opened his life to God, he'd clung to this tiny part of him, holding on to his guilt so tightly that he'd denied himself the intimacy that he craved with the Father.

He didn't want that distance anymore. *"Forgive,*

and you will be forgiven." He'd understood that much from the Scripture in the Book of Luke. But now he finally understood that to have the kind of relationship he longed for with God first and then with the woman he loved, he had to finally forgive himself.

Half of January had already ticked away and tax season was in full force by the Monday morning when Hannah received a strange summons for a meeting at Hickory Ridge. It had to have something to do with Deacon Littleton's question before the holidays, she surmised. Otherwise, they never would have called on her.

Still, she'd been unsettled by the odd sound in her father's voice when he'd phoned, asking her to join the meeting. Was the discrepancy more serious than the head deacon had let on?

Unbidden, her thoughts flashed to another time and a different meeting in the church conference room. Andrew and Serena had been there, facing down the Deacons' Board and accusations of sexual impropriety, all to protect Hannah's secret a few days longer. Though she had no sin to confess this time, a sense of foreboding tripped up her spine.

Nothing appeared too out of the ordinary at first, even the Michigan State Police patrol car that sat in the parking lot alongside several other cars. Trooper Brett Lancaster occasionally stopped through while he was patrolling the perimeter of GM Proving Grounds where they connected Livingston and Oakland Counties.

But the second police car, this one from the Milford

Police Department, gave her pause. Something was very wrong, and from the tone of her father's voice, it had something to do with him.

Call Todd, a voice inside her immediately suggested, but she pushed aside the thought. She didn't know anything yet, and even if she did, her only reason to phone him would have been to lean on him, and she had to believe she was stronger than that. She was probably just being silly to consider calling him.

A rumble of voices emerged from the conference room as soon as she passed through the church entrance. She knocked on the door before pulling it open. A sense of déjà vu struck her like a sudden wave of nausea.

The painting of Jesus surrounded by children still hung above the fireplace in the room where, to describe the lighting as poor would be considered an understatement. All nine deacons were in their regular places along the long dark wood conference table. Reverend Bob and Andrew were seated at the end of the table on metal folding chairs.

The cast would have been the same as from that play five years before except for the addition of building contractor Rick McKinley, who'd recently filled the vacancy on the Deacons' Board, and two uniformed officers, representing different police agencies.

"Oh, Hannah, we're glad you're here."

The greeting came from Deacon Littleton, but Hannah couldn't help glancing at her father instead. Reverend Bob had folded his hands in a prayerful pose, but his eyes were open. Though his glasses had slipped down his nose, he made no effort to push them back in place. How old and pale he looked, as though he'd battled the world and lost.

Her pulse raced, and it was all she could do not to rush to her father and demand to know what was wrong.

"Hannah," Deacon Littleton said to draw her attention back to the center of the table.

"What's going on?"

The head deacon glanced around the room before he spoke. "Do you remember the bookkeeping problem I mentioned to you a few weeks ago? Well, my mistake didn't turn out to be a mistake."

"I don't understand." Thoughts rushed at her in a hailstorm that allowed no time for weighing conclusions. What did this have to do with her or her father?

Deacon Littleton gestured toward Milford Police Chief Pete Conyers, who picked up the conversation from him. "Hannah, there appears to be a widespread case of embezzlement involving several of the church accounts, including the building fund for Hickory Ridge's Family Life Center."

She shot another glance at her father, who still stared at his gripped hands. Panic tasted acidic in her mouth. Could her father have— No. She dismissed the thought before it had a chance to fully form.

"There has to be some mistake."

"Unfortunately, there isn't." Brett spoke this time, his expression grim. "My gut told me something was wrong. I should have listened…"

Hannah drew her eyebrows together as another thought struck her. "You don't think I—"

Andrew came to his feet, shaking his head to stop the direction of her question. "No, Hannah, we don't. Look, we're not making ourselves clear. We've asked you here for two reasons—your familiarity with the church accounts and your acquaintance with Olivia Wells."

"Olivia?"

"Also known as Olivia Wilson, Olivia Wilder and Olivia Whiting," Chief Conyers said, looking up from the spiral-bound notebook in his hands.

"Are you serious? What kind of money are we talking about?"

Deacon Littleton glanced down at the printed list of figures in front of him. "As close as I've been able to tally it so far, about twenty-five thousand dollars."

Hannah blinked. To some families in the wealthy suburbs of Detroit, a figure like that was a nice bonus after a healthy sales season, but to a small church, where every dollar had to be stretched to keep the black columns from becoming red, it was a fortune.

"She is also wanted for questioning in connection with embezzlement cases at the Presbyterian church in Brighton, a Methodist one in Okemos and a tiny Baptist congregation in Dansville," Chief Conyers continued.

"I knew she looked familiar that first time I saw her at Bible study," Brett said, shaking his head. "But I just couldn't connect the sweet lady at church with the police sketch on the bulletin board I passed every day at the *Brighton Post.*"

Andrew lowered into his seat next to Reverend Bob. "Come on, Brett, give yourself a break. She fooled us all."

Several of them glanced at Reverend Bob then, but if he noticed at all, he didn't give any sign of it. He was the one who had been fooled most of all, and Hannah wished with all her heart she could take away her father's pain.

Brett, clearly in his role as Trooper Lancaster now, stood and paced the room.

"Hannah, when is the last time you saw Olivia Wells?"

"Uh, it must have been at church yesterday." She thought for several seconds. Come to think of it, Olivia hadn't been there. If she'd noticed it at the time, she would have thought it odd. Olivia had become one of the most regular attendees in the last several months. "No, that isn't right. I think it was a week ago Sunday."

Brett cleared his throat. "And what about you, Reverend?"

The minister started at being addressed directly. "I'm sorry. What did you ask?"

"When is the last time you saw Olivia Wells?"

"At church on January eighth. She said she would be away a few days visiting some extended family."

Brett wrote something down in his notebook. "Did she happen to mention where these family members lived?"

"Outside Lansing, I think, but that could mean anywhere, couldn't it?"

"Yes, it could, but it could also mean that Olivia hasn't skipped the state yet."

"And that she really might be from Michigan," the police chief chimed in. "The suspect certainly tried to stay close to home while committing her alleged crimes. All the embezzlement cases occurred within a fifty-mile radius. We'll check the NCIC database— that's the National Crime Information Center—and see if we come up with any hits."

Andrew, who had stepped to the rear of the room to refill his foam coffee cup, turned back to the rest of them. "That one's simple. She took a chance that leaders of the different churches in the region didn't hang out together and share notes, and she was right."

All those in the room nodded and murmured over that, probably feeling by varying degrees guilt over the lack of ecumenical fellowship that had allowed someone to continue these crimes for so long.

There would be more questions to follow: how much they knew about Olivia Wells outside church, where she lived and who else resided with her, what she did during her off-hours from the church office. The last question turned back to the man who had remained strangely quiet throughout the meeting.

"Bob, you will make yourself available for further questioning, won't you?"

Reverend Bob nodded to Chief Conyers but didn't meet his gaze. The whole situation struck Hannah as terribly unfair. Olivia had been the first woman her father had taken any interest in since her mother's death.

How cruel she had to be to take advantage of struggling churches and a man who'd done nothing but give of himself to those who needed him.

When the meeting was finally over and most of the others had filed from the room, Hannah turned back to her father, who sat staring out one of the room's two narrow windows. Andrew paused at the doorway and caught Hannah's attention, but she motioned for him to go ahead without her.

As she approached her father, he smiled up at her, but the expression didn't reach his eyes.

"Are you okay?"

"I wouldn't call it my best day."

"What would you call it?"

"A day when I'm glad God is here to catch me."

He reached his right arm across his body to rub his left shoulder.

"Here, let me do that." She kneaded his shoulders that felt frailer than she remembered. Was it a sign of adulthood to realize her father was just a middle-aged man rather than some larger-than-life hero?

"Thanks, honey." He shifted so that her hands fell away from him.

"This could all be a big misunderstanding, you know."

"It could be."

But they both knew it probably wasn't. Olivia's absence was at the very least suspicious.

Instead of saying more, Bob glanced at his watch. "Shouldn't you be getting back to work?"

"Is that an excuse not to talk about it anymore?"

"Possibly."

"But you'll call me if you need anything?"

"Of course."

As reluctant as she was to leave, Hannah crossed to the door she'd entered. Her father returned to gazing out the window or, as she suspected, talking open-eyed to his God.

From the pulpit and in his home, Reverend Bob had always taught Hannah not to hate, but she was having an awfully hard time following his example. If Olivia Wells was guilty of the crimes they suspected, she'd hurt Hannah's father in ways beyond his social life. She'd attacked the church community he'd loved and nurtured. She'd struck him right in the heart.

With her arms stretched like an airplane, Rebecca took timid, wobbly steps along a balance beam that rested squarely on the gymnastics center's padded flooring. Todd willed her on each step as he watched through the window of the viewing area. Her parents cheered when she reached the end and took the six-inch jump to the ground.

Their little girl beamed, looking like a true gymnast in that sparkly little leotard she'd been begging to wear every day until her gymnastics class began. At least one of them was having fun.

He glanced sidelong at Hannah, who had pasted on a smile and was giving their daughter the two-thumbs-up.

"You can tell me what's wrong now," he told her.

"There's nothing—"

"And you can stop denying it, too."

Hannah opened her mouth and then closed it again. Her shoulders slumped, and she covered her face with her hands, exhausted eyes peeking out between her splayed fingers.

"There was a problem at church today. It's a mess, and it involves my dad."

"Yeah, I heard."

Dropping her hands, she turned her head to face him. "You knew?"

"Brett wanted to know the last time I'd seen Olivia. He filled me in on the details."

"If you knew what was wrong, then why have you been pressing me from the moment you picked us up?" She straightened in her seat and turned back to stare through the window into the gym.

"I wanted to hear it from you. We've seen each other every day since New Year's, and we talk on the phone at least once a day while we're not together. With something as important as this, you might have called."

If she'd noticed the annoyance in his voice, Hannah pretended she hadn't. "I just didn't want to bother you at work. I planned to tell you about it tonight." She pointed to the glass. "Oh, look what Rebecca's doing now."

His jaw tight, Todd turned his head back to look through the window. Their daughter was standing on top of a cube-shaped foam form, while her instructor helped her into the correct position to do a forward roll down the incline of the triangular-shaped form next to it. With assistance, she managed the move on the first try.

Rebecca lifted both arms in the air, having mastered a gymnast's "ta-da" bow just as easily. Again, her parents clapped, presenting the perfect, happy fan club.

As soon as they stopped applauding, Todd leaned in close to Hannah. "You know I would have come."

"I know. That's why I didn't ask."

Couldn't she understand that it was exactly why she should have asked? *Need me,* he wanted to shout, and yet he hated how pitiful that sounded. Hannah's family was in crisis. She had enough to worry about without having to balance on eggshells not to hurt his feelings.

"How's your father doing?"

"Probably better than I would be in the same situation." She paused to glance at Rebecca, who was taking her turn swinging on the thick rope that dangled from the ceiling, before she turned back to him.

"For Dad's sake, I hope this turns out to be a mistake. If it's true, if Olivia really did this to him and our church, I pray that she's arrested and convicted."

"I hope your dad isn't hurt by the scandal. He helped Olivia get her job, didn't he?"

"Yes, he did," she said, her hands coming up to rub her temples. "I don't know what Dad and I will do if…" She let her words trail away as if she couldn't bear to complete the thought.

"You mean what *we* will do, as in all of us, right?" Todd didn't realize how harsh his comment sounded until she drew her eyebrows together and stared at him.

"What?" She shook her head as if to clear it. "Oh. Right. That's what I meant."

"Of course."

Hannah turned her attention back to the class, but Todd couldn't stop replaying the conversation in his mind. She planned to *tell him about it,* but he wasn't invited to get involved. Maybe her comment wouldn't have bothered him so much if distance weren't so endemic to their relationship. He was allowed to spend time with Hannah and Rebecca as long as he stayed at arm's length. He could love them as long as he didn't get close enough to hurt them.

Chapter Fourteen

Hannah frowned at Todd's profile as they went through Rebecca's bedtime routine two hours later. He'd been brooding all night, through the ride home from gymnastics, their daughter's bath and her bedtime prayers. Hannah had tolerated his moodiness at first, but now she'd reached her limit.

She dropped a kiss on Rebecca's brow, tucking the blankets under her chin. "Sweet dreams, honey."

On the other side of the bed, Todd snuggled up to his daughter, cheek to cheek. "Sleep tight, Becca."

Their last smiles of the night were for their daughter as they shut off the light. As soon as they closed the bedroom door, Hannah tugged on Todd's arm, directing him toward the kitchen. Once inside it, she pulled the pocket door closed and whirled on him.

"What in the world is the matter with you?"

"Were you really going to *tell me about it* tonight?"

He slumped into the seat at the kitchen table where

he'd hung his coat earlier and stared up at her, accusation in his eyes.

"What are you talking about?"

"You would tell me, but you never had any intention of letting me help you or your dad."

She blew out an exasperated breath, dropping into the seat across from him. Usually, she would have sat next to him so he could reach for her hand, but she wasn't in the mood to be touched. She could tell by the way he studied her chair that her move hadn't gone unnoticed.

"It's not that big a deal. We didn't need—"

"That's right. You don't need me or want to need me. That would be too much risk for you."

Hannah blinked, startled by his accusation. "I don't understand you. Don't you think I have enough to worry about right now without you bringing this up?"

His gaze narrowed, making him look far angrier than he should have been for something as trivial as her neglecting to call him after the meeting at church.

"When do you suggest I bring it up?"

"Sometime when my family isn't in an uproar."

"Your family? *Your* family?" His voice had climbed an octave by the second time he said it. "You're *my* family. Can't you see that?"

She shook her head, exasperated. "Of course I see that."

"Then would you finally let me in?"

It was Hannah's turn to be angry. "Let you in? That's all I've been doing since you came back here. First, into my house, then into our lives and into my heart. What more do you want?"

"Ever since I came back, you've been holding me just out of reach. The thing at church today is just the symptom of a larger issue. It's just like before, when you were pregnant. You wouldn't let me help then, and you won't let me now."

"This situation isn't anything like before. It isn't really even about me."

"Isn't it?"

"No. And besides, I haven't been holding anything back from you. I even told you that I love you." She heard the sharp, accusatory tone in her voice, but she couldn't help herself. Didn't he realize how much that admission had cost her?

"But you don't trust me."

She opened her mouth to dispute his words, but he raised a hand to stop her.

"Sure, you trust me to show up for dinner on Friday and not to be late when I have plans with Rebecca, but when it comes to your hopes and your fears, you're not willing to let yourself fall into my arms. You're afraid I won't catch you." He gripped the edge of the table with both hands. "You don't trust me at all."

"Can you blame me? You left!" she shrieked. "I'll probably never be able to trust you completely."

The second the words were out of her mouth, Hannah was sorry she'd spoken them, even sorrier that she'd ever thought them. But she couldn't take them back now that the words hung between them, heavy and permanent. Worse than what she'd said, no wishing could change the fact that she'd spoken the truth. He would have to understand that, but they could find a way to work past it, couldn't they?

Todd flinched as if she'd struck him with her hand rather than her words. The wound, she surmised, would have been less grievous if she'd just hit him.

Planting his elbows on the table, he leaned his head against his folded hands and squeezed his eyes shut. He stayed that way for what felt like an eternity. Though a few minutes before she'd avoided touching him, she longed to reach across the table, squeeze his hands between both of hers and tell him they would find a way to make everything all right. They had to.

Only when he looked up at her again, pain and resignation so clear in his eyes, did she begin to realize what she'd lost.

He shook his head, a self-deprecating laugh emanating from deep in his chest. "I had all these great ideas when I came here. I would win you back, and we would begin the life together that I had imagined before you'd even realized we were more than friends."

Hannah drew in a sharp breath. "We can still have all that…in time. That doesn't have to change."

He lifted his gaze to meet hers but only briefly before he reached back for the coat hanging on the chair behind him. Out of the pocket, he produced a satiny white box. "I've been carrying this ridiculous ring around in my pocket since before New Year's."

Turning it toward her, he popped open the box, revealing a sparkling marquise solitaire diamond. Hannah coughed, swallowing the sob that scaled her throat with angry claws. He stared at the ring, the fluorescent kitchen light fluttering over its facets, before he snapped the box shut and stowed it in his pocket.

Todd smiled, perhaps at a pleasant memory, though certainly not at her. "I even had it with me during that New Year's Eve service at church. I knew it was too soon, but I had to buy it anyway. It was this silly, romantic notion that I'd be beginning the new year with our future all planned out."

Without looking at her, he continued, perhaps as much to himself as her. "That night, I was so tempted to slip off the pew and propose right then and there in the candlelight. The only thing that stopped me was this sense that God was telling me to wait."

He reached behind him again, his hand closing over the pocket where the tiny box rested. His lips formed a grim line. "I wonder what the return policy is on engagement rings."

Hannah's eyes burned, and her chest felt as if a horrible weight had been placed on it, cutting off her oxygen, her hope. "Please don't give up on us, Todd," she begged, hearing the desperation in her own voice.

"But don't you see? I have to. For my own survival." Todd reached across the table and squeezed her hand just once before pulling away. "You never really forgave me for deserting you, even though we both wanted to believe it when you said you had. You aren't able to forgive me, and I can't live with the truth that you can't."

"But, Todd, I have…" Hannah let her words trail away, surprised by how unconvincing she sounded.

"I know you tried. Just as I tried to earn your forgiveness. But I finally realized something." His smile was a sad one. "Forgiveness from someone you've hurt is like God's forgiveness. It isn't earned. It's a gift."

Tears filled Hannah's eyes and spilled over before she could control them. "I'm so sorry."

Again, he touched her hand, just a brief squeeze of comfort that he might have offered any friend who mourned as she did now. "I'm sorry, too. But I can't marry you. We'll always have some kind of relationship as Rebecca's parents, but I can't build a life with you."

"I…love…you…Todd." Each word seemed to emerge on its own wave of agony. Impotent words, their message moot.

He covered his face with his hands, and when he pulled them away, his eyes were damp, his raw pain visible.

"And I love you. Until a few weeks ago I believed that knowing you loved me would be enough for me." He shook his head as if to emphasize how wrong he'd been. "But now I realize that I have to have your forgiveness, too. I have to have your trust."

Todd backed his chair from the table and stood. Clearly, he recognized as she did that there was nothing else for them to say. Hopelessness filled her at the thought of the impasse they'd reached. Loving Todd wouldn't be enough to keep him with her. Another truth, though, produced a fresh ache inside her: Her heart had been broken by her own unwillingness to bend.

Reverend Bob stared at the computer screen the following evening, Sunday's sermon still no more than a title on the screen. "The Tithe." But how could he give the annual message to his congregation about sharing their financial gifts and talents with the church community when he was responsible for bringing in someone who'd stolen from them?

He had a headache and his shoulder was hurting again, but neither of those things should have surprised him after the day he'd had. Even though no one had mentioned the investigation since yesterday's meeting, he could think of nothing else.

He'd been holed up in his office all day with the intention of writing his sermon, but he'd gotten no further than looking up the word "tithe" in his concordance and searching for fresh Scriptural references in what church members often considered a tired topic. Already, it was past five, but he wasn't in any hurry to leave the security of his office and to face the uncertainty of his life.

The sound of a file drawer closing in the next office told him that Andrew was making a long day of it, as well. The youth minister wouldn't press him, but Bob felt comfort in knowing his friend was there if he needed him.

"Lord, what am I to do?" he whispered. "How do I make this right?"

It wasn't as if he expected an immediate answer. God

always answered prayer in His own time, and His answers were perfect. Still, the tick of the flashing curser on the computer screen seemed to taunt him like a series of questions marks with no answers in sight.

His office suddenly felt so warm. He peeled off his gray wool sweater and unfastened the top button of the shirt he wore beneath it. With his handkerchief, he dabbed at the perspiration dotting his brow.

This crime, and he was beginning to be convinced that a crime had been committed, would hurt the Hickory Ridge community so deeply. Where would they come up with another twenty-five thousand dollars to replace the missing funds?

He would claim responsibility for the fallout. He was the one who'd introduced Olivia to the Deacons' Board and convinced its members she would be a good candidate for the church office position. Her résumé had been solid, but he'd been too distracted by her physical beauty and her passion for God to check her references. That beauty had been on the surface only, and even her faith had probably been only a masquerade.

Had he helped her at least in part because he wanted to impress her so she would see him socially? He shook his head. No, Olivia had definitely been the one to pursue him from the day she'd first shown up at the church's Christian Singles United program and then at morning Bible study.

At the time, he'd found her interest flattering. Now that he knew her real motivation for visiting Hickory Ridge, it only compounded the humiliation he felt for letting the whole church community down. Perhaps he deserved the shadow of suspicion this case would cast on him and on the ministry he'd built at Hickory Ridge over the last fifteen years.

He would probably be forced to resign now. Who could blame the deacons for making that decision? Would he ever be called as a head minister of a church again?

The last thought was too much for him to take. His eyes and nose burned as emotion clogged his throat. He removed his glasses and would have wiped them with his handkerchief, but his left hand felt strangely numb. No rubbing seemed to awaken his slumbering fingers. He was still staring down at it, still wondering at the sensation when he felt a strange pressure, like a weight, on his chest.

Realization settled just as heavily as that weight. He clutched his chest. *Lord, help me.*

"Andrew." He couldn't tell if he'd yelled or only whispered, but he tried once more. "Andrew…help."

The computer screen, the unfinished sermon and the portraits on his desk wavered in and out of focus. He had to get help…reach the door…call to Andrew. Bob struggled to his feet, holding himself steady by gripping the edge of his desk. He could do this. He was close to the door. So close.

Turning away from his desk, he took that first step toward the door. There wouldn't be a second step as darkness swept up from the floor and swallowed him whole.

* * *

The phone rang the moment Hannah entered her kitchen with four plastic grocery bags slung over her arms. She planned to let it ring and deny yet another telemarketer the opportunity to invade her home during the dinner hour, but Rebecca got to the phone first.

"Hello." The little girl shook her head. "No, this is Rebecca.…My mommy?…Yeah, she's here."

"Here, honey, let me talk, okay?" she said, making a mental note to warn her daughter about answering the phone, and especially about identifying herself to strangers. She accepted the handset, mentally preparing herself for the sales pitch about a great new long-distance plan or a low rate on a home-equity loan, but the voice on the other end of the line startled her.

"Hannah, it's Andrew."

She drew in a breath. Had Olivia been arrested? Had the embezzlement been more far-reaching than they'd first imagined?

"What's wrong?" she immediately asked, though Andrew had phoned to check on her and Rebecca many times over the years. His tone didn't suggest a social call.

"It's your dad. We think he's had a heart attack."

"Heart attack?" A million thoughts—all dark and devastating—slammed through her mind at the same time. "Is he—"

"No, he's alive, but I think it's serious."

"Is he conscious? Is he asking for me?"

"He's been going in and out. Before the ambulance

arrived, I had to use that portable defibrillator we had installed at the church last year."

"Andrew, does that mean—"

"Now, Hannah, we don't know anything yet. You just need to get to West Oakland Regional Hospital as soon as possible. The ambulance just left to take him there."

"I'll be there." Either she was experiencing an overwhelming sense of calm or she was in shock, but she suspected the second. She backed to the kitchen table and slumped into one of the chairs. She couldn't just sit there. She needed to move, and yet she felt paralyzed. Details needed to be handled, but for the life of her she couldn't list them in her mind.

"Hannah, do you want me to have Tricia take Rebecca? Or do you need me to call Todd for you?"

"No, I'll phone him, but thanks."

Only after she ended the call did she realize she'd answered only one of Andrew's questions, and it should have surprised her which one, but it didn't. Without bothering to wonder whether after last night she should ask, she dialed his number. She had to. She needed him.

He answered on the second ring.

"Todd."

"Hannah, is that you?"

"Yeah, um, I have some bad news."

"Tell me. What is it?"

"It's Dad. They think it's a heart attack."

"Oh, I'm sorry, honey."

"This can't be happening. He's only sixty."

"He'll probably be fine," Todd tried to assure her.

"I have to leave for the hospital. Do you think you could—"

"Are you at home?"

She glanced at the bags of groceries still sitting on the counter, the ice cream already beginning to melt. "Yes, but—" She didn't even know *but what*. Her whole world was cloudy, and the only thing that seemed clear was that she'd made the right decision to call him.

"Stay where you are. I'll be there in five minutes."

Chapter Fifteen

He'd made it in four. Hannah smiled at the thought when little else had given her any cause for happiness since she'd arrived at West Oakland Regional four hours before. Todd had driven her to Commerce Township after showing up at her house so quickly that she'd only had time to toss water on her face and wrestle Rebecca back into her boots and coat.

He'd insisted that Hannah was in no shape to drive, and only now did she realize he was right. She couldn't have navigated the village streets and twenty-miles-per-hour zones on the way to the hospital without him.

In fact, she couldn't have handled any of the details without him—from registering her father in the emergency room to contacting relatives to planning for Rebecca's care.

She hadn't thought about any of those details again until now, not since she'd glimpsed her father in that hospital bed with so many tubes and wires and monitors attached to him. Not when the hours that followed were filled with tears, prayers and uncertainty.

But in this moment of clarity, she allowed herself to recall all of the help Todd had given her, even after all the awful things they'd said to each other the night before. When the ground had seemed to be shifting beneath her, he'd been a solid rock, calmly suggesting that she give him her keys so he could take Rebecca home where the child could sleep in her own bed.

Todd's help and her silent admission that she couldn't handle the situation alone would have terrified her a few months ago—or even a few days ago. Self-reliance had once mattered more to her than self-respect. But she felt a strange sense of relief in accepting Todd's help. It felt good to leave the details in his capable hands.

She couldn't allow herself to read too much into Todd's kindness. Just because he'd reached out to her didn't mean he would be able to accept her on her terms—conditions that even she could no longer justify. Todd was a good man. He would probably have done as much for anyone in need, but still her heart squeezed with gratitude. He'd caught her when she was falling, despite the fact that she'd hurt him in ways she couldn't even imagine. If only she could be the kind of woman Todd deserved.

A creak from the door at the back of the chapel drew Hannah from the lonely place her thoughts had ventured. Mary Nelson stood in the spray of brightness seeping into the softly lit chapel through the open door.

"Hannah, sweetie. The nurse was looking for you. She said you could go back in and see Bob."

"Is he conscious again?" Hannah asked as she straightened in her seat and brushed at the smeared mascara beneath her eyes.

"She didn't say. They only give reports to family members."

Those words drew Hannah's gaze back to the woman standing just inside the door. Mary was watching an arrangement of lighted candles on the far wall. She looked so sad. Standing up from the short pew where she'd been sitting, Hannah crossed to her dear friend and placed her arm around her shoulder.

"That nurse obviously doesn't know us then." If anyone was family to her father, Rebecca and her, it was Mary. No lack of blood ties could change that.

"I'll let you know as soon as they tell me anything, okay?" she said as she stepped back from her.

"Thanks. I'm sure the others will want to hear, too. Nearly twenty church members are in the waiting room."

"Dad would be so embarrassed by the fuss." She paused before adding, "And humbled by the concern."

Mary's smile couldn't quite take the sadness from her eyes. "He's too used to being the one in the hospital waiting room, drinking bad coffee and leading the prayers." She pointed to the door. "You should go on now. He shouldn't…be alone."

Her voice broke then, anguish she'd been holding back all evening breaking through the cracks of her control in a near-silent sob. That hopeless sound tore straight to Hannah's heart, and she gathered Mary into her arms.

"Why didn't you tell my father?"

"Tell…him…what?" Mary asked in a muffled voice into her shoulder.

"Oh, come on, Mary. That you love him."

Mary pulled back and gripped Hannah's forearms. Behind her glasses, the older woman's eyes were red rimmed, their usually shiny brown color had lost some of its luster. "How did you know?"

Hannah chewed her lip. Perhaps this wasn't the best time to mention that anyone paying attention—clearly her father couldn't be counted in that number—would have noticed how Mary lit up the moment Reverend Bob walked into the room. Her interest hadn't been as obvious as Olivia's, but then Mary's affection was more sincere.

"Maybe people carrying around secrets have a special connection with others who have secrets," Hannah told her.

"Maybe."

Hannah watched as Mary tightened her tan cardigan sweater around her body and retied its belt at her waist. She could relate. Hannah hadn't been warm since the moment Andrew had called her with the news.

"My father is blind if he doesn't see how wonderful you are and how wonderful your lives would be together."

"Thanks, sweetie."

"He's going to be okay, you know," Hannah said, surprised to find herself reassuring the other woman when she wished she could be that certain.

Yet Mary nodded as if she had enough confidence for the both of them. "God and I have been talking about that all night."

Arm in arm, the two women moved down the hall to the waiting room. Several church members came to their feet as they entered the room. Andrew was the first to reach them, but others—Rick and Charity McKinley, Charity's mother, Laura Sims and Deacon Littleton—gathered around them.

"You'll want to check at the nurses' station," Andrew said. "They're looking for you. I think they're ready to give you an update."

He indicated for Hannah to wait for a second while he helped Mary settle back into her seat, and then he went with her to the nurses' station. She wouldn't allow herself to think that the youth minister was there to support her in case she had devastating news.

"Miss Woods?" the nurse asked when they reached the desk. At Hannah's nod, she continued, "I'll page the doctor if you can wait here for a minute."

"I'm sure he's going to be fine, Hannah," Andrew told her while they waited.

She smiled at having received the same assurance she'd just given Mary, but something from earlier struck her, and she studied Andrew. "You said before you had to use the portable defibrillator on my father. Did his heart stop?"

"No, but his heart rate went crazy. The defibrillator did what it was supposed to do, though. When I put those pads on his chest, the machine said he had an irregular heartbeat, and then it shocked his heart. After that, the EMTs arrived." Andrew stared down the empty hallway, appearing lost in his thoughts.

"Thank you for saving my father's life."

He turned back to her. "God just made sure I was in the right place at the right time."

"Then thanks for listening to Him."

The doctor arrived with an update. After a string of four-syllable medical terms, Hannah managed to gather that her father had been given a "clot buster" drug and was heavily sedated. Though he would soon be moved to the Cardiac Care Unit, Hannah was allowed a few minutes with him in the Emergency cubicle.

Leaving Andrew to update the others on his condition, Hannah passed beyond the locking metal doors leading into the E.R. Inside the curtained cubicle, she found her father much as he'd been when she'd seen him briefly hours earlier.

It was so strange to see her big, strong daddy reduced to merely human under the hospital's unforgiving fluorescent lights.

"Oh, Dad…"

Again, heat rose behind her eyes. She'd already watched one parent die, had sat back as a helpless spectator while her mother wasted away, her sweet spirit losing its battle before her body succumbed. Hannah couldn't imagine how she would survive if her father died, as well.

She shuffled to the chair across from the narrow hospital bed that looked like a heavily padded ambulance stretcher. Pulling the chair close to the bed, she sat and reached over to lay her hand atop her father's.

"Come on, Dad, wake up."

Hannah waited, expectant, but this was real life, not the movies. Reverend Bob's eyelids didn't even flutter. Then her gaze moved to the IV stand and the morphine drip, and she remembered. At least he wasn't in pain. The monitor next to the bed showed the zigzag evidence of his heartbeat, and his chest continued to rise and fall in a steady rhythm.

The tiny room blurred. She didn't bother brushing away the tears that trailed down her cheeks. Without closing her eyes in case her father chose that moment to emerge from unconsciousness, she whispered a prayer.

"God, please lay Your healing hands on my father. Please heal his heart and send him home to us." She couldn't bring herself to pray for God's will in the situation when she feared that His will might have been something very different from her own. "His work here isn't finished yet, and we don't know what we'll do without him."

She hadn't breathed the word *amen* yet when the words from Philippians 1: 6, one of the many Scriptures her father had encouraged her to memorize over the years, drifted through her thoughts. "'He who began a good work in you will carry it on to completion until the day of Christ Jesus,'" she recited softly, hoping her father would hear the Scriptures he loved and open his eyes.

His chest continued to rise and fall in its steady rhythm. Hannah shrugged and shook her tired head. It had been worth a try. Coming up from her seat, she leaned over her father and kissed his lined forehead.

She stepped to the edge of the curtained area and glanced back at her father once more, but she felt none of the earlier anxiety at having to leave him for the short while until he could be moved to Cardiac Care. He was only resting, and the doctors were making sure he wasn't in too much pain. *He who began a good work in you.* The Scripture gave her comfort when everyone's platitudes, including her own, hadn't helped. It felt as if God was telling her that her father's work here really wasn't finished. Finally, she felt some cause to hope.

Hannah stumbled into her apartment Friday night, operating on only the fumes remaining after a three-day adrenaline rush. As she shrugged out of her coat, several snowflakes broke away from her scarf and fluttered to the floor. Strange since she hadn't noticed it was snowing. The roads were probably slick tonight, but she hadn't noticed that, either. God's hand must have been on her car for her to make it home at all.

Her back ached between the shoulder blades from too many hours spent keeping vigil next to her father's bed, but the rest of her body felt numb. She could barely distinguish the first day from the third in her memories as each worry, each prayer and each moment of fore-boding melded with the ones before.

She would have been there even now if Mary hadn't promised to stay with her father through the late-night hours and insisted that she go home and get some sleep.

Hannah wondered if she would be able to sleep, anyway. After all the nightmares she'd witnessed while wide-awake, would she be able to take a chance at succumbing to her dreams? She'd witnessed too much of life's frailty and fleetingness not to wonder what would happen when she closed her eyes.

Hannah glanced around the empty rooms of the apartment. It felt so small, so unwelcoming, when a few days earlier she'd thought of it as home. In the corner, Rebecca's dolls, except for Miss Gabrielle, sat too neatly atop the toy box, awaiting the girl's return. The special doll had served as their daughter's companion all week while she'd spent her nights with her father and visited with other church members while Todd worked during the day.

She wondered if she should have asked Todd to bring Rebecca back tonight instead of waiting until morning, but then she worried if that would have been more for her benefit than her daughter's. And she suspected that even if Rebecca were in the next room sleeping, Hannah would still have been prowling around the dark apartment, trying not to crawl out of her skin.

Guessing that she might feel better if she ate, she shuffled to the kitchen and pulled open the refrigerator door. Eggs, lunch meat, fresh vegetables and milk lined the shelves. Todd had put her groceries away that first night and had been adding items to the refrigerator since then. Once again, he'd handled the details when she'd been too overwhelmed to do more than put one foot in front of the other.

Too bad her stomach was rolling so hard that she couldn't consider eating any of the food he'd supplied. She couldn't pull her thoughts away from her father, who was still battling his way back to health, though he'd already made it through the darkest hours.

For his part, Reverend Bob had dozed away most of the hours of his crisis under sedation, only occasionally having a few lucid moments to hear of the clot busters and the angioplasty that had cleared the blockage in his heart and the life changes that would be necessary to continue forward.

Perhaps more distressing than watching her father had been serving as witness to Mary's silent vigil. Each time Reverend Bob had awakened, Mary had been among those nearby, but she'd taken care to stay on the periphery.

What did it feel like to have that kind of regret? To love in secret, to pine alone? The ironic thought wedged a new ache inside her heart. Hannah knew that regret intimately. She'd lived that secret love, she'd pined, and when she'd had the opportunity to live that love out in the open, she'd been too scared to risk her whole heart. For that, she'd lost everything.

Hannah tried to push those useless thoughts aside as she changed into a pair of oversize sweats and climbed into bed. But her thoughts chased her in the darkness. She'd made so many mistakes out of anger and fear. Though the anger had faded, she'd clung to the fear.

She was so tired of being afraid. She was tired of letting that fear run her life.

Hannah sat straight up in bed and climbed out from beneath the sheets. She wouldn't be getting any sleep anyway. Straightening her sweats, she threw her hair into a ponytail and pulled on her coat. In the bottom of her purse, she dug around for her keys. She knew it was late, but it was long past time to set things right.

Chapter Sixteen

A knock at his front door awakened Todd, but that wasn't saying much when he'd done no more than toss and turn for the past three nights on the lumpy sofa in his town house apartment. He'd even sacked out early tonight, hoping to catch up on his sleep, but that only gave him time to count every paint drip and shadow on the ceiling and to notice how bare and pitiful his walls looked.

After untangling himself from his makeshift bed, he staggered toward the door in his Detroit Tigers sweatshirt and plaid lounging pants. He rubbed his aching neck and wondered why he'd ever bought that couch. It made a better torture device than a cozy place to kick back and watch TV—and an even worse bed. But he'd given up his bed to his little girl.

When he opened the door, Hannah stood on his stoop, her pulled-up hood keeping her face in shadow. His thoughts and his pulse raced.

"What is it, Hannah?" He shook his head, trying to

find some clarity. "Is your dad okay? Did something happen? I thought he was doing better."

She pushed past him into the apartment. Until she swept the door closed behind her, Todd hadn't even noticed the snow blowing in on his bare feet.

"Dad's fine," she assured him as soon as she'd pulled off the hood. "Well, as fine as someone can be with a damaged heart and bruises all over his legs from doctors routing catheters through his arteries."

"Remind me to never have a heart attack."

"Never have a heart attack."

"Thanks."

"You're welcome."

Hannah smiled as she removed her coat, but her effort couldn't quite brighten the exhaustion dulling her eyes. She looked bone-weary, with blue-gray crescents beneath her lower lashes. At least she looked comfortable, dressed in sweats just like the ones she used to wear when they were teenagers.

"Why are you here, Hannah?" As soon as her eyes widened, Todd was sorry he'd asked. She would probably leave now, and no matter what he'd said before, that was the last thing he wanted. "Did the police catch up with Olivia? Or did you want to see Rebecca? I can wake her up if you want me to."

She shook her head, not indicating which question she was answering. "No new news that I'm aware of. Oh, I wanted to thank you for taking care of Rebecca and for the food. For everything." She leaned her back against the door, folding her arms and rubbing her hands over her upper arms.

"That was nice of you to call Grant. He came by the hospital to see Dad and me."

"He's your friend" was all Todd was able to say. He'd known Hannah needed a friend these last few days, and he'd wanted to make sure someone was there for her if he couldn't be.

Hannah nodded. "He said you were really nice to him and invited him to come back to church." At his shrug, she continued, "Grant said you're a nice guy."

Todd could only imagine what those kind words had cost Grant, but the blessing of Hannah's friend didn't matter now that everything had changed.

Stepping farther into the living area, she lowered her gaze to the sofa, covered with a tangle of blankets and bedsheets. "Oh, I woke you. I'm sorry. I can go."

"I don't want you to go. I just want you to tell me why you came."

"To talk," she said finally.

She glanced at the couch again. He'd made sure Hannah hadn't seen it messy like this each morning when she'd picked up Rebecca. But he hadn't been prepared for her visit this time.

"That had to be so uncomfortable. You gave up your bed for Rebecca?"

"She's my child."

She nodded, as if she, too, understood that no sacrifice was too great for their daughter.

"Anyway, I was planning to buy a bed for Rebecca's room when she visits, but I didn't get the chance before…"

Hannah met his gaze, obviously not missing that he'd referred to his guest bedroom as Rebecca's room.

"Are you sure you don't want me to get her up? She'd probably love to see her mommy."

"I don't want to wake her, but I would like to look in on her if you don't mind."

Waving his hand for her to follow him, Todd led the way down the short hallway past the spare room that would soon be their daughter's to the slightly larger master. In the center of the big bed that had been his one self-indulgent purchase—aside from the big-screen TV in the living room—Rebecca looked so tiny, so young and precious. She lay with her knees tucked under her body and her backside pressed up in the air.

"She used to sleep like that when she was a baby," Hannah whispered in the doorway.

"You probably loved watching her sleep."

"I did." Hannah slipped inside the room and dropped a kiss on their daughter's silky head. Then she followed him out of the room.

"Why didn't you just sleep in there with her?" Hannah said as they reached the living room. "There's certainly room."

"I didn't want to wake her by coming in later. I did lie down with her each night, just until she got to sleep."

An unsettling silence fell over the room then, while Todd held back his questions and Hannah didn't offer any answers. Their lives had changed over the last few days since Reverend Bob was hospitalized, but nothing could change the things they'd said to each other before all this happened. They couldn't take those things back.

"You said you wanted to talk," Todd said when he couldn't stand to wait any longer. "Here, let's sit."

He hurried over and ripped the sheets, blankets and pillows off the sofa, dropping them unceremoniously in a pile on the floor. He lowered himself onto the cushion, and Hannah followed his example, but instead of beginning, she sat gripping her hands together.

"Do you want me to take Rebecca for the rest of the weekend?" he prompted. "I can take her next week, too, if that will help you out. I don't have any vacation yet, but I can probably work something out. Whatever you need—"

"I need my best friend."

She said it so softly that Todd wasn't sure he'd heard her right at first. A lump suddenly filled his throat. He coughed into his hand. What was she saying? He needed to be cautious for his self-preservation. Could he be only a friend when his heart wanted to be all things to her—a husband, lover and a friend?

But even his misgivings couldn't stop him from drawing the only woman he'd ever loved into his arms and offering her whatever comfort his sturdy shoulders could provide. She didn't sob as he'd thought she might, but she held on tightly, her fingers pressing hard into his back.

It felt so good holding Hannah in the circle of his

arms. He'd thought he would never hold her again, and his arms had ached from the loss.

He couldn't help himself. As he breathed in the floral scent of her hair and felt her clinging to him as if he possessed all the answers to her life's questions, he couldn't help wishing for impossible things, things he'd told himself he could live without.

For the longest time, neither said anything, and they simply rocked back and forth on that lumpy sofa.

Though he longed to hold her just like that forever, Todd forced himself to set her back from him. She'd clearly come with something to say, and he wanted to give her the chance to say it.

"I've had a lot of time to think lately," Hannah said when he was convinced she would never tell him what was on her mind. "Though I spent time praying for my father's recovery, there were still plenty of empty hours for me to get my head on straight."

"I always thought it looked pretty straight before." Even now, even in this quiet, serious moment, he couldn't help teasing her. Humor was part of who they'd always been together.

She rolled her eyes at him, but she still smiled. "Thanks. Watching my dad go through all this was like a roller-coaster ride. First, the heart attack. Then the clot buster drug opened the blockage. Just when everything seemed okay, it reclotted, and they had to do an angioplasty to break it up again.

"It was hard enough for me to watch my father in pain that way. But then seeing Mary going through it was worse. I don't know…" She let her words trail away, shaking her head.

Todd sat back in his seat and crossed his arms as he tried to follow along in her story. Clearly she wanted him to read between the lines, but he was missing the point.

"Mary Nelson was there?" Come to think of it, other church members had been watching Rebecca when Mary was her regular sitter.

Hannah nodded. "I felt so badly for her. It was so sad. She wouldn't leave Dad's side. She just sat there regretting the things she'd never said and wondering if she would ever have the chance to say them."

"That had to be tough."

Todd understood what it was like to second-guess decisions. *If I knew then what I know now…* But he decided not to lie to himself. He would have chosen to return to Hannah every time, and he always would have risked any pain for the chance to know his daughter.

"I don't want to do that," Hannah said, drawing him back from his thoughts.

"To do what?"

"I don't want to live with that kind of regret. Not anymore."

Todd shook his head with more sorrow than determination. "Hannah, so much has happened between us. A lot of things we can't change no matter how much we wish we could."

"Please," she said, turning her shoulders so she faced him as they sat. "Please let me try."

Todd braced his hands on the edge of the sofa, his chest feeling tight. Though he wished it were different, nothing had really changed between them. She needed him to hear her, so he would listen, but he couldn't allow himself to settle for less than his heart needed to survive. "Go ahead."

"I've thought a lot about what you said about God's forgiveness and our forgiveness. You're right. It is a gift. One I never gave you."

As she spoke, Hannah gripped her hands together and squeezed her left thumb so tightly that it turned red at the tip. "I never really forgave you for leaving me, though I told myself—and you—I had. I was lying to us both."

"No, Hannah. You believed it, so it wasn't a lie."

"But you saw right through me."

One side of his mouth lifted. "Well, not at first, but…" He was tempted to say *not soon enough,* but he couldn't wish away a single minute of the sweet hours of his oblivion. Knowing was better, he kept telling himself, hoping he would eventually believe it.

"I just couldn't see it. And I couldn't forgive the way God forgives. Completely. He doesn't hold a grudge, but I did. I was wrong."

Todd couldn't stop himself from reaching for her hands and curving his fingers over her clinched grip. "We both were. About a lot of things. But we were just kids. We made mistakes."

Hannah gently pulled her hands from his, tucking them under the sides of her legs. "Even if we could have used that as an excuse then, it doesn't work now. For me, it was more than just not forgiving. Blaming you was easier than facing the truth that most of the misery in my life I'd brought on myself."

Todd opened his mouth to interrupt her, though he wasn't sure what he would say to defend her when she'd spoken the truth. His instinct was to protect her even if she was wrong.

"No, let me say this. It's long past time."

Closing her eyes, she held her index fingers together like a church steeple and pressed the bridge of her nose to the point at the top. Finally, she spoke again. "I was wrong to keep Rebecca a secret from you. At first, I did it because I was angry, and then the secret became like a trap I'd built and then couldn't escape from it."

"Once everything was going smoothly again, it was probably just easier not to make waves," he said.

"I kept waiting for the right time, and I know now that if you hadn't returned, that *right time* would never have come."

Though Todd had often suspected that was the case, he still ached inside having heard it spoken aloud. "I can't imagine not knowing her."

"And her life would never have been the same if she hadn't gotten to know her daddy. She…loves you." Her voice broke as she spoke the word *love*.

He could still hear Hannah's timid voice when she'd confessed that she loved him, and it still hurt to realize that love wasn't enough.

"I'm so sorry, Todd. And I'm proud of the father

you've become. All those hours and minutes I've stolen from the two of you I can't give back." Tears were
tracing down her cheeks unchecked.

"Honey, thank you for saying it, but I forgave you a
long time ago."

Though she'd been staring at her hands in her lap,
Hannah lifted her gaze to meet his. "It took me a lot
longer than you to reach that place, but I want you to
know that I'm finally there. Forgiveness is a gift, and
I'm giving you mine right now. All of it."

"Are you sure?"

"I'm sure."

If he questioned at all whether she was sincere, he
had only to look in her eyes. Her pain and regret was
clear.

Todd drew in an unsteady breath. He'd waited, he'd
hoped and he'd mourned when hope had disappeared.
And now Hannah sat there before him, the woman
who'd possessed his heart since before he'd even become a man, offering him the thing that mattered most.
She'd gift wrapped her promise for him and tied it with
a bow.

Without hesitation, he leaned forward and folded
Hannah in his arms again. It felt like coming home,
holding her there, with her cheek resting against his
shoulder, her tears dampening his sweatshirt. He sensed
that God had formed his arms at least in part for the
honor and responsibility of holding her.

For several seconds, they clung together, giving and
receiving comfort. Finally, Todd pulled away and looked

into her tearstained face. He slid his hands down her arms and then reached up and brushed away her tears with his thumb.

"I love you, Todd. Do you think there's a chance for us...after everything?"

His heart squeezed as he stared into her pleading eyes. Even after all this time she still didn't know how deeply he loved her. Wordlessly, he showed her, first by gently taking her hands and pulling her to her feet and then by pressing his lips to hers.

Never had a kiss felt so perfect. He didn't know if it was possible to squeeze a lifetime of hopes and dreams into a single kiss, but he tried to convey it the best he could.

"I love you," he breathed against her skin.

Tracing her hands over his shoulders, Hannah clasped them at his nape. She smiled up at him, her eyes shining, and then stood on tiptoe to kiss him. It felt as if she was giving him a message of her own— one of promises made and promises kept.

When the kiss ended, he touched his cheek to hers. A chuckle bubbled from deep inside him. "Look at us. We've had to travel so far to get to each other."

Hannah pulled her head away so she could look up at him. "Some of us farther than others."

"At least we can tell our grandchildren I flew around the world to win you back."

"Grandchildren?"

Todd couldn't help grinning. It was so nice to lighten the mood after the intensity of the conversation they'd just had and the week they'd just survived. "You think we should worry about raising the children before we make plans for the grandchildren?"

"Children? As in plural?"

"Is that a problem?" He waved his hand to dismiss the subject. "We don't have to make decisions about the future right now. It's too early for such serious discussions."

Hannah shook her head, looking at him with a confused expression. "Too early for what?"

"Too early Saturday morning." He pointed to the wall clock that read half past midnight.

"Oh, I should be getting home," she said, taking another step back from him.

Automatically, both of them turned to look at the door, and just as quickly Todd realized he wasn't ready for her to leave. If she left now, he would wonder if her visit tonight had just been the one pleasant dream on his uncomfortable couch bed.

"I don't know about you, but I'm starved." He waited until she looked back at him before he spoke again. "How about I make us some breakfast?"

She lifted a shoulder and lowered it, probably preparing to decline, when her belly growled. Pressing her hand against her stomach, she gave him an embarrassed grin. "I wasn't hungry earlier."

"Sounds as if you are now. Besides, are you in a hurry to go out in that?" He stepped toward the front window and gestured for her to join him.

Outside, a new blanket of snow had transformed

Milford into one of those scenes on a Christmas card, and the snowfall didn't appear ready to taper off anytime soon.

"I guess I'm not in a rush. It's pretty out there, though."

Todd slipped his arm around her shoulder, and they watched the snowflakes flutter to the ground for a few minutes longer. The snow was pristine, still unmarred by foot traffic or turned to gray sludge by automobile tires and exhaust. Under the streetlights, some of the flakes on the ground sparkled like diamonds.

That fresh snow reminded him of the new, tentative relationship they were forming inside the glass. Without the stains of past mistakes, everything felt new.

Chapter Seventeen

Reverend Bob blinked a few times before finally opening his gritty eyes. The space around him blurred first and then settled into an equally confusing clarity. It was dark outside his low-lit patient room, and several snowflakes clung to the window.

He wasn't sure how long he'd slept this time or whether he was better off now than he'd been the last time he'd awakened. Now that the medication was wearing off, his body felt as if he'd experienced the unfortunate end of a battle with a steamroller. At least the doctor had warned him to expect some soreness.

Turning his head slowly toward the side of his bed where his IV stand rested, he was surprised to see he wasn't alone. Mary Nelson slumped in a chair next to the bed rails, her head at an awkward position on the backrest. She would be sore when she awoke, but she dozed so peacefully that he hated to awaken her.

He reached for his glasses from the bedside table and glanced at her again. She was a handsome woman

with a youthful face, an ever-present smile and a con-
tagious joie de vivre, but there was an extra sweetness
about her while she slept.

Come to think of it, Mary had been around a lot the
past few days, always seeming to be with Hannah when
he'd awakened. He couldn't have been more grateful to
her and the other church members for helping Hannah.

Suddenly, her eyes fluttered open.

"Hi," he said when her gaze came to rest on him.
"You again."

She straightened in her seat and patted her dark hair
nervously though its no-nonsense, short style appeared
tidy as always. "Yes, me."

"Where's Hannah?"

"I sent her home for some sleep."

"Thanks. You look like you could use some sleep,
too."

Mary waved away his suggestion with her hand. "I'm
fine. I just wanted to help out."

"You've been hanging out at the hospital a lot this
week. You must really like the antiseptic smell."

He'd meant it as a joke, but she looked embarrassed,
refusing to meet his gaze. Bob drew his eyebrows together. Maybe the painkillers hadn't worn off as much
as he thought, and he was still under a medicated haze.

"I just couldn't leave, not when you were lying there,
when you still didn't know."

"Know what?" As soon as the words were out of his
mouth, he realized he knew the answer to his own question. A hundred tiny things—inconsequential things

like an offer of help on the church Christmas Decorating Committee and kind words after some of his sermons—added up in his thoughts. Though not overt like Olivia's attention, Mary had shown her affection in simple ways, and he'd been oblivious to it all.

"I'm sorry. I didn't realize."

She smiled. "People are blind sometimes."

"I suppose they are." He smiled back.

Strange how he knew Mary so well, as a church member, a friend to his daughter and to him and a child-care provider to his granddaughter, but until now he'd never seen her as a woman. A kind and compassionate woman. She'd fit so seamlessly into their lives that he'd never noticed.

He noticed now.

"In all these years, you've never told me about your late husband," Bob began, suddenly wanting to know everything about her.

"George has been gone ten years now."

Mary's eyes took on a faraway look that Bob recognized. Others probably had read it in his eyes hundreds of times over the past few years. Clearly, Mary remembered her late husband the way Bob cherished his memories of Deborah. Mary would understand that a part of his heart would always belong to his late wife.

They continued talking in hushed voices for another half hour, sharing stories of Bob's daughter and the happy life Mary and George had lived together though they'd never been blessed with children. Occasionally, Mary would offer him ice chips or a cup of water. The conversation was simple and unrushed as the two of them got to know each other for the first time…all over again.

Hannah followed as Todd led the way to the kitchen. She should have gone home, especially with all that snow blowing around outside. But she couldn't bring herself to leave him now, not when they had just found hope for a new beginning. Besides, it was only breakfast. She would leave right after they cleaned up the dishes and after she cleared the snow off her car.

"What are you hungry for?" Todd said as he peered into the shelves of his refrigerator. "Eggs? Pancakes? I make a mean omelet."

"No Belgian waffles or a soufflé?"

"You're testing your short-order cook's abilities here." His head popped up from behind the refrigerator door. He kicked it closed, balancing eggs, a stick of butter, green peppers, mushrooms and tomatoes in his arms. "The fridge is looking pretty bare except for these."

"What a coincidence. I just happen to have a craving for scrambled eggs with tomatoes, mushrooms and green peppers."

"Then we're set." He lowered his collection of food to the kitchen counter and gestured for her to sit at the glass dinette.

"But I can help."

"You can also sit there and watch me."

Todd collected a mixing bowl, cutting board and frying pan from the cabinet and pulled a knife and a whisk from the drawer next to the stove. He seemed utterly focused on his culinary duties, as if their conversation from twenty minutes before hadn't fazed him a bit.

How could he concentrate on dicing vegetables and melting butter when their relationship had just taken a huge step from impossible to probable? Hannah was glad she wasn't cooking because she would have sliced off a finger or two along with the tomatoes.

"You're awfully quiet," he said, not looking up as he poured the egg mixture into the pan.

"Just thinking."

"Care to share?"

"Not especially.

He shrugged, but even in profile, she could tell he was smiling. Though she suspected he was enjoying her discomfort a little too much, she couldn't help smiling with him.

Just as the toast popped and Todd moved the frying pan from a heated burner to a cold one, Hannah heard a sound behind her. Rebecca stood in the doorway wearing her yellow, footed pajamas and a frown. She rubbed her eyes and squinted under the fluorescent kitchen light.

"Daddy? Mommy? Is it morning time?"

When her daughter crossed the room and climbed into her lap, Hannah brushed Rebecca's messy hair back from her face. "Hi, sweetie. Did we wake you up?"

"It smells funny," Rebecca said, wrinkling her nose.

"Green peppers. I guess a smell like that is better

than an alarm clock." Todd grinned when he turned back from the stove with two filled plates in his hands. He set one plate in front of Hannah and the other at the empty space beside her.

"Honey, we'd better get you back to bed. It's too early for you to be up."

Rebecca pointed to the dark bread sticking out of the toaster. "I want to eat breakfast, too."

Todd pointed to his colorful egg dish. "Want some?"

"Yuck."

"We like it." He looked conspiratorially at Hannah. "Do you think we should share some of our toast with her?"

Hannah squinted her eyes, trying to appear deep in thought. "I don't know. Only if we put jam on it, I guess."

"Ooh, jam."

Soon the three of them were seated around the table, enjoying an early-morning family breakfast. Hannah found herself memorizing the sights, sounds and tastes of it. This was what she'd hoped for. This was how she'd always imagined family life to be, and if it wasn't really like that, she hoped she wouldn't wake up from her dream.

When they had taken the last bites of eggs and Rebecca had enough jam on her face to spread on a third piece of toast, Todd cleared away the dishes, refusing any help. He made quick work of loading the dishwasher and then opened a cabinet to put away the spices he'd used.

Sitting opposite Hannah, on her knees so she could reach the table, Rebecca planted her elbow on the table and rested her heavy head on her hand.

"Do you want me to carry you back to bed?" Hannah's heart warmed as she watched her sleepy little girl. In another couple of years, she wouldn't even be able to carry Rebecca to bed. She hoped that time passed as slowly as possible.

"Can Daddy carry me?" the sleepy voice asked.

Quickly, Todd turned his head back from the sink where he'd returned to wash his hands. He appeared startled that Rebecca had chosen him over her mother, even for this small privilege. His gaze met Hannah's, and he waited.

In the span of a heartbeat, she smiled. His expression softened, as well.

"Sure, I can take you, honey." He turned away from them, digging his hand into the spice cabinet once more. "But I need to do one more important thing first, okay?"

"Okay, Daddy."

Hannah turned back to the counter, not seeing anything left to finish. Then Todd approached the table with a satiny white box in his hand, and she knew. She drew in an unsteady breath. But when his lips curved upward and his gaze connected with hers, all of her nervousness drifted away.

Never breaking eye contact with her, Todd lowered himself on one knee and opened the box in his hand. Again, the lovely solitaire winked out at Hannah, not long ago a painful reminder of broken promises and now a symbol of a lifetime commitment.

"Hannah, I've loved you ever since I can remember."

"Daddy, are you and Mommy going to get married now?" Rebecca asked, suddenly bright-eyed instead of drowsy.

Hannah started, having forgotten momentarily that this tender moment was for a crowd of three rather than two.

Todd looked up from his position on the floor and held the white box high enough for Rebecca to see. He lowered his voice and winked as if he were sharing a big secret. "I'm getting ready to ask her."

The preschooler grinned as if she'd had her second Christmas in a month. Hannah looked back and forth between the man she loved and their child. Perhaps it wouldn't be as private as some proposals, but it certainly would be as memorable.

"As I was saying," Todd began again, "I've always loved you, even before I understood what love was and what it meant to put someone else's needs ahead of my own. Though our mistakes pulled us apart, God has led us back to each other and given us the most awesome responsibility of raising our child.

"I would love to do that with you, side by side. Will you please be my wife and finally make our family complete?"

"Please, Mommy, say yes." Rebecca had climbed down from her chair on the opposite side of the table, and now she knelt by her father on the linoleum floor.

"Yeah, please, Mommy, say yes," Todd chimed in with a grin.

"Well, you two are pretty persuasive. I think I'll have to say…yes. Definitely. Absolutely. I want more than anything to spend the rest of my life with my best friend. How's that for an answer?"

"Good enough for me."

Todd pulled the ring out of the box and, taking her hand, slipped it on her finger. Still holding that hand, he leaned forward and touched his lips to hers in a kiss of commitment.

"Me, too." Rebecca snuggled between them.

Todd stood and, with one arm, scooped up a giggling Rebecca, while extending his other hand to pull Hannah to her feet. For several seconds, the three of them stood there in the kitchen, in a tight group hug.

Hannah inhaled the sweet scents of the two people in the world she loved most. Her feelings must have shone in her eyes because Todd smiled down at her. "You see, I told you I would ask when the time was right."

She reached over and brushed Rebecca's hair back from her face. "I think you picked a perfect time."

When Todd released her, Hannah glanced down at the blindingly beautiful ring on her finger and then up at him. "I thought you said you were planning to return the ring."

"It's a better story to say that I decided not to return it, knowing that in the end we would be together, but the truth is this week was so crazy for all of us that I didn't get around to taking it back."

"Go with the first story. The grandkids will like it better."

"Grandkids?" He glanced at the child still propped on his hip.

"Ah, but we should probably focus on our children before we worry about that next generation."

"Children? As in plural?" he said, repeating her words from earlier.

"We'll have plenty of time to discuss that later."

But Rebecca, who had rested her head against her father's shoulder, once again close to dozing, suddenly straightened. "I want a baby brother."

"Is that so?" Todd tweaked her nose.

"And a dog," Rebecca added.

"Oh yes, the dog." He turned back to Hannah to explain. "Max got a dog after Tricia and Brett were married."

He ruffled Rebecca's hair. "How about we worry about that after your mom and I are married? But first we get to plan a big church wedding."

Rebecca was cheering, the baby brother and the dog forgotten for now, but Hannah stared at Todd in shock.

"A big church wedding? Don't you think it would be inappropriate—"

Instead of answering her, Todd gave his daughter a conspiratorial glance, the side of his mouth pulling down in a frown. "I'm going to have to convince your mommy to have a big party, so I'm going to take you back to bed first, okay?"

Rebecca didn't argue with that, so he washed her

face and left the room with her, staying gone only long enough to tuck her in and kiss her good-night again. But that was plenty of time for Hannah's secret dreams of a perfect, elegant church wedding to resurface. She'd understood that they were just dreams, each time she'd awakened from them, still humming the organ postlude. Was it right for a young mother to still wish for all that pomp and ceremony?

When Todd returned to the kitchen, he jumped back into the conversation before she had her argument ready.

"Are you saying it's inappropriate for me to marry the woman I love in front of God and all our friends?"

"Maybe something small and in the parsonage would be better. It wouldn't be so—"

"So what?" Instead of waiting for her to answer, he pressed forward again. "Is that the wedding you've always dreamed of…at the parsonage?"

She shrugged and then finally shook her head. "But it's different for us—"

"Is it?" He reached for her hand on the table. "Aren't we a young couple in love, ready to make lifetime vows before God?"

She wanted to believe, wanted to smell the floral scent filling up the sanctuary, wanted to speak those precious words and feel her Lord's blessing on their vows. "I just don't know if we should."

"Can you name a single member of Hickory Ridge who would object to us making our wedding a big celebration for the whole church?"

Hannah said nothing, only pressing her lips together and trying not to smile.

"Okay, I take that back." There wasn't a church around that didn't have a judgmental member or two, and he'd already met Laura Sims at Hickory Ridge. "Would *most* of the members of our church be thrilled to celebrate with us?"

"Yes, but—"

"Then we should give them a reason to celebrate."

"I don't know."

"Sure you do. What would Reverend Bob want you to do?"

"He would tell me to follow my heart."

"Are you going to?"

And suddenly Hannah realized that she was going to do just that. She knew deep in her heart that Todd was the man God intended for her. She wanted her whole church family to be a part of the beginning of their life together. Love like theirs deserved to be celebrated.

"We'd better get busy. We have a wedding to plan."

Chapter Eighteen

Hannah stood outside the glass separating the vestibule from the sanctuary on the first Saturday after Valentine's Day. On the other side of the glass, a wedding scene very different from the one she'd pictured in her dreams was unfolding. Different but just as nice.

In keeping with the season of love, the church was adorned with red and white roses and white tapered candles. Small red hearts blended with the fluffy bows on the ends of the pews.

She brushed an unsteady hand down the front of her ivory satin wedding gown, her fingers smoothing over the stitching from one of the appliqués just below the fitted waist. It was a beautiful dress, and she should have been feeling like a princess wearing it, but the band around her neck felt too tight and the seams on the bodice itched.

"Do you need some sneakers? Are you going to make a run for it?"

Hannah looked up to find Serena Westin standing

before her in her crimson-colored bridesmaid gown. The dress had been let out to allow for Serena's advanced pregnancy, but she still looked darling in it, her skin rosy and glowing.

"I'm not running anywhere. But you can if you need the workout." Hannah fussed with her veil, only managing to make it go cockeyed on her head.

Tricia Lancaster stepped forward to right the thing, resecuring the headpiece with the bobby pins Hannah had pulled loose. "What are you so nervous about, anyway? This wedding has been a long time in coming."

"Too long, but this isn't exactly how I pictured it." She pointed to the glass doors leading to the outside, where a mid-February snowstorm raged. Though most of the guests had arrived only in the last fifteen minutes, their cars were already covered with a thin layer of snow that would build during the next few hours of the wedding and dinner reception.

Steffie Wilmington looked up from where she was adjusting the strap of the satin sling-back shoe that matched her bridesmaid's dress. "Look in there. This storm didn't stop anybody from getting here."

"At least Roy and Sharon got here a few days early," Hannah said. "I would have hated it if their flight had been delayed and they'd missed their son's wedding."

"Are you kidding?"

Hannah turned to see the woman she'd just spoken of had come up behind her. "Oh, hi."

Her future mother-in-law leaned close and air-kissed Hannah so she wouldn't muss her hair. "We wouldn't have missed this for the world." She scanned the vestibule, looking past three of Hannah's bridesmaids. "Where is that beautiful granddaughter of mine?"

Hannah looked around, for the first time noticing her daughter's absence. "Oh, no, where is she?" Wedding or no wedding, she should have been watching. What if something happened to their little girl all because she was distracted?

"Relax, sweetie," Charity McKinley called out as she emerged from the ladies' room in her bridesmaid's dress. Charity stood holding hands with Rebecca, in her frilly, crimson flower girl dress, and Max Williams, in his tiny ring bearer's tux. "Remember, I was supposed to take the junior members of the wedding party for a last potty break before the ceremony."

"Oh. Right."

"Hi, Nana," Rebecca called out, rushing into Sharon McBride's arms, as if they'd known each other years rather than days.

Sharon gave her granddaughter a squeeze. "Oh, it's time for the usher to seat the mothers—" She wore a pained expression when she turned to Hannah. "Oh, I'm sorry, sweetheart."

"It's all right." But that wasn't completely true. Hannah hadn't realized how putting on this gown and preparing to stand before these people with her own daughter would make her miss her mother more intensely than she had in years. Her father was here and she should have been satisfied with that, especially after how close she'd come to losing him, too, but part of her still longed to share her wedding day with her mother.

Sharon cocked her head and studied Hannah for a few seconds as Tricia handed her son, Max, his ring bearer's pillow and gave Rebecca her basket of flowers. Finally, Sharon drew Hannah aside, and lowered her voice.

"You have to be missing your mother a little today. I didn't know her well, but she seemed like a kind woman. I would never want to try to replace her, but I want you to know that I would feel privileged if you would think of me as a mother to you as much as to my son."

Hannah's eyes burned, and she sensed her nose was in danger of dripping right on her wedding gown. Still, she pressed her cheek against Sharon's. "Thank you."

Because she couldn't say more and not be the first to cry at her wedding, she left it at that. The organist chose that moment to begin playing "The Wedding Song," by John Lennon, and she had to hold her breath to keep from smearing her makeup.

"Well, ladies, how about we get started with this little shindig," Andrew said as he came out to be with the wedding party. He indicated for Sharon to go with the usher waiting to escort her down the aisle.

At the same time, the door at the right front side of the sanctuary opened, and Reverend Bob, Todd and his father, whom he'd chosen as his best man, filed out and took their positions at the front of the church.

And suddenly the day became perfect after all.

Todd. Always Todd.

In his black tuxedo, he looked more handsome than in her best dream, though he was already tugging at his tight collar. He turned toward the back of the church, seeking to see her face from behind the crowd in the wedding party.

She was so grateful to him for seeking her out in the first place, even when she'd been perfectly content to hide behind her wall of anger and secrets. He'd given his heart to her, and she felt so unworthy of the gift.

Her gaze drifted to the other man she loved most. He still looked frail, far from the robust hero of a father she'd either known or imagined. But it warmed her heart to see him standing there in front of the altar, his well-worn Bible clasped between his hands. First, he stared down at the book as if in prayer, and then his gaze traveled up and off to his right. Hannah didn't have to look far to discover who held his attention. There'd been a lot of secretive glances lately.

Mary sat discreetly in the fifth row, needing no place of honor as the minister's lady friend. Hannah didn't even have to worry that her dad would overdo it on her wedding day, not with Mary keeping a careful watch over him. Like Todd and Hannah, her father and Mary had been given another chance at love, and Hannah was so pleased to see that they saw it for the gift it was.

As the music changed for the processional, grooms-men Roy McBride, Grant Sumner, Rick McKinley and Brendan Hicks took their places next to the bridesmaids. Hannah couldn't be more pleased that Todd included her friend in the wedding party. It was another reason to love Todd, as if she didn't have enough already.

Andrew stepped next to Hannah and tucked her hand in the crook of his arm.

"Thanks for standing in for my father, Andrew."

He smiled down at her. "I'm honored." He helped her lower the blusher of her fingertip veil over her face.

Hannah watched as her sweet little girl traveled down the aisle, scattering flowers from her basket and somehow managing not to run to her daddy as he stood near the altar. She was pleased that the paperwork had already been filed for Rebecca to eventually carry her father's name.

"Doesn't it seem like we've traveled an awfully long journey to get here since that night when you and Serena let a scared, pregnant teenager cry on your shoulders?"

"Sometimes the best destinations are found at the end of long journeys." Andrew turned back to watch little Max and the rest of the wedding party proceed down the aisle.

Again, the music changed, and the crowd rose and turned back to the entry where only Hannah and her escort stood.

Hannah turned to her friend once more before she took her first step toward the man she loved. "And sometimes that end is just the beginning."

Todd's heart squeezed and his throat clogged as he watched his bride marching to him in a lovely gown that still paled next to her beauty.

To him. He loved the way that sounded. After all this time, after all the emotional miles she'd traveled away from him, they were there together walking toward their future.

Hannah smiled at him, her gaze never leaving his, as she continued down the aisle. As much as he'd longed for the years they could already have spent as husband and wife, he wondered if he would have cherished the gift of a life with her if it had come easily.

When they reached the front of the aisle, Andrew placed Hannah's hand in Todd's, and they turned to face Reverend Bob. Instead of beginning with the "dearly beloved" speech they'd all come to expect, the minister stopped and lifted the front of Hannah's veil to kiss her on the cheek.

"Over the years, I've married dozens of couples," he said, slipping one hand inside his Bible to hold his place. "But this is a once-in-a-lifetime experience for me as a father. I get to marry the daughter of my heart to the young man who claimed her heart so many years ago."

Reverend Bob turned his attention to his Bible. Soon Todd found himself speaking the words he'd only dreamed about in the five years he'd waited to return to Milford and to Hannah. She smiled at him, love so clear in her eyes that Todd could barely recite his vows without his voice breaking.

So this was what it felt like when a man received everything he'd ever wanted. He was amazed and humbled by it.

Todd turned to his father, who lowered the wedding

band with five tiny inset diamonds into his hand. Holding her left hand, Todd slipped the ring on her finger.

"With this ring, I thee wed."

Once she'd slipped the plain gold band on Todd's finger, Reverend Bob told him he could kiss his bride. As Todd touched his lips to hers, he felt a wonderful peace of completion, as if God's will finally had been done.

"I love you," he murmured against her mouth.

Hannah's lips turned up. "Right back at you," she whispered.

The minister motioned for Rebecca to join her parents before the altar. "I would like to present to all of you for the first time, Todd and Hannah McBride and their amazing daughter, Rebecca. And I'm not the least bit partial here, either."

Applause and laughter broke out in the auditorium, and even a few whoops could be heard coming from the back of the room. For a relationship that had borne its share of sadness, it was only right that its new juncture would begin with cheers.

Hannah wiped the last bit of white buttercream frosting off her cheek from the smear Todd had given her when he'd fed her their wedding cake.

"Sorry about that," Todd said, using a napkin to help her. "I didn't know you were going to turn your head."

"A likely story," she said with a grin.

All across the open area of the church's Family Life Center, guests sat at tables eating huge quantities of homemade dishes that church members had provided for the reception. Indulgence was the order of the day, and that was even before they reached the cake with its white roses and intricate piping. Of course, there were several heart-healthy selections for her father to choose from, and he had been allowed the tiniest sliver of wedding cake.

"Are you sharing any of that cake?" Brett Lancaster asked as he swiped three plates from the table. The state trooper took a few steps away before turning back to Hannah.

"Did Reverend Bob tell you the good news?"

"What news?"

"Police caught up with Olivia yesterday in Jackson. She'd already picked a little Friends church there as her newest target and had just started a job in the church office."

Hannah shot a worried look at her father who was sitting at one of the red cloth-covered tables next to Mary. News of Olivia's arrest hadn't been too hard on his heart apparently if he could find that much to laugh about this afternoon.

Todd came up behind Hannah and dropped kiss on top of her head. "Did I hear someone say good news?"

"They've arrested Olivia," Hannah explained before turning back to Brett. "Any word on the missing money?"

Brett shrugged. "We're unlikely to recover much of it for any of the churches. Olivia apparently had a gambling problem, and she was always looking for a new mark to pay her debts."

"That's too bad," Todd said.

"Are you serious?" Hannah asked, but then she shook her head. "Sorry. Forgiveness is a bit tough for me. I didn't know whether you knew that about me or not."

Todd stepped up beside his wife and took her hand. "I've heard tell."

Several members of the wedding party crowded around them then.

Julia Sims was the first to speak up. "Brett, are you sharing your good news with everyone who will listen?"

Hannah looked at the other church members quizzically. She felt guilty enough about her eye-for-an-eye reaction to news about Olivia's arrest without having to see her fellow church members have a veritable celebration over it. "He's already told us about the arrest."

Brett shook his head, drawing Tricia under his arm when she came near him. "We have more good news. We're expecting!"

Hannah looked back and forth between them. "You, too?"

Todd stepped forward and shot his hand out to Brett. "Congratulations, buddy. What do the kids think about it?"

Tricia shrugged. "Rusty Jr. and Lani are pretty excited about it, but Max isn't sure how he feels about giving up his position as the youngest."

"They're all excited that we're going to have to move to a bigger house, though," Brett added.

Steffie seemed to be getting a big kick out of the

announcement. "You see, I told you not to drink the water."

"I know," Tricia said, shaking her head and feigning a sad expression. "I should have listened."

"You two," Steffie said, pointing to the church's newest pair of newlyweds, "had better watch out. There's something in the water at Hickory Ridge."

Hannah scanned the crowd standing around her. At nearly full-term, Serena rested her hand on the small of her back and had removed the shoes from her swollen feet. Charity and Rick were standing next to them, and unconsciously Rick's hand had moved to splay across his wife's slightly rounded tummy. Tricia didn't show at all yet, but a new life grew in her womb, as well.

"Okay, I'd better avoid all the church water fountains," Hannah said, trying to keep a serious face. "Should I worry about the water we use to make the coffee, too?"

"I say bring on the church's water." Todd didn't even bother to hide his amusement. "I want to fill up our house with babies, and we should get on it as soon as possible."

As if he hadn't realized how the comment would sound until it was out of his mouth, Todd ended his statement with an awkward "oh." He covered his eyes with his hand.

More laughter filled the room.

"All-righty then," Rick said with a mischievous grin. "Sure glad we got the Family Life Center finished. It sounds like there's going to be a population explosion at Hickory Ridge, and there would be no place for all the Sunday School classes."

Finally, the party began to wind down. Hannah allowed Todd to draw her into one of the classrooms for a quick kiss. She was nervous, but she couldn't wait to be alone with her husband, consummating their life together, this time with God's blessing.

As the kiss ended, Todd pressed his forehead to hers. "Are you happy, Mrs. McBride?"

"Very."

"Are you sorry we waited so long?"

She shook her head. God's timing was perfect, and this was the perfect time for her family to be together.

Todd bent to kiss her again, but a passel of children zoomed through the room, playing hide-and-seek as they often did in the classrooms with their removable room dividers.

"Mommy, Daddy, why are you in here?" Rebecca stopped long enough to ask.

"Just taking a minute to be alone."

That seemed to satisfy her, so she ran off again.

As soon as the room was empty, Todd sneaked another kiss.

"We'd better get back to our reception," Hannah said finally. Hand-in-hand they returned to the main room, earning a round of applause from their guests.

When Hannah looked over at her father, he was smiling.

"Does this seem like a dream to you?" Todd whispered in her ear, his warm breath tickling her neck and ear.

Hannah nodded, smiling. "If it is, I don't ever want to wake up."

"We'll keep dreaming together," he promised.

"I don't have to dream anymore, when all of mine have already come true."

* * * * *

Dear Reader,

Isn't forgiveness a wonderful thing? Whether it's the gift we receive from each other or the perfect absolution that God provides for all of us who ask, it cleanses, heals and restores. But for so many people, true forgiveness is so hard to give. My character Hannah Woods happens to be one of them.

Writing this story has felt like a long journey home for me. The characters of Todd and Hannah first came to me when I was writing *A Blessed Life* (October 2002), and I always knew I would return to them. Readers, too, seem to have found a special place in their hearts for the unwed teenage mother, Hannah, and have asked when I would be telling her story.

The characters in each of the Hickory Ridge sequels have become so real to me over the years. I love returning to visit with them, and hope readers find as much enjoyment on these return visits.

I love hearing from readers and may be contacted by visiting my website at www.danacorbit.com or by regular mail at P.O. Box 2251, Farmington Hills, MI 48333-2251.

Dana Corbit

REQUEST YOUR FREE BOOKS!

2 FREE INSPIRATIONAL NOVELS
PLUS 2
FREE
MYSTERY GIFTS

Love Inspired

YES! Please send me 2 FREE Love Inspired® novels and my 2 FREE mystery gifts (gifts are worth about $10). After receiving them, if I don't wish to receive any more books, I can return the shipping statement marked "cancel." If I don't cancel, I will receive 6 brand-new novels every month and be billed just $4.49 per book in the U.S. or $4.99 per book in Canada. That's a savings of at least 22% off the cover price. It's quite a bargain! Shipping and handling is just 50¢ per book in the U.S. and 75¢ per book in Canada.* I understand that accepting the 2 free books and gifts places me under no obligation to buy anything. I can always return a shipment and cancel at any time. Even if I never buy another book, the two free books and gifts are mine to keep forever.

105/305 IDN FVW5

Name _____ (PLEASE PRINT)

Address _____ Apt. #

City _____ State/Prov. _____ Zip/Postal Code

Signature (if under 18, a parent or guardian must sign)

Mail to the **Reader Service:**
IN U.S.A.: P.O. Box 1867, Buffalo, NY 14240-1867
IN CANADA: P.O. Box 609, Fort Erie, Ontario L2A 5X3

**Are you a subscriber to Love Inspired books
and want to receive the larger-print edition?
Call 1-800-873-8635 or visit www.ReaderService.com.**

* Terms and prices subject to change without notice. Prices do not include applicable taxes. Sales tax applicable in N.Y. Canadian residents will be charged applicable taxes. Offer not valid in Quebec. This offer is limited to one order per household. Not valid for current subscribers to Love Inspired books. All orders subject to credit approval. Credit or debit balances in a customer's account(s) may be offset by any other outstanding balance owed by or to the customer. Please allow 4 to 6 weeks for delivery. Offer available while quantities last.

Your Privacy—The Reader Service is committed to protecting your privacy. Our Privacy Policy is available online at www.ReaderService.com or upon request from the Reader Service.

We make a portion of our mailing list available to reputable third parties that offer products we believe may interest you. If you prefer that we not exchange your name with third parties, or if you wish to clarify or modify your communication preferences, please visit us at www.ReaderService.com/consumerschoice or write to us at Reader Service Preference Service, P.O. Box 9062, Buffalo, NY 14269. Include your complete name and address.

LIDIR12

LARGER-PRINT BOOKS!

**GET 2 FREE
LARGER-PRINT NOVELS
PLUS 2 FREE
MYSTERY GIFTS**

Love Inspired

Larger-print novels are now available...

YES! Please send me 2 FREE LARGER-PRINT Love Inspired® novels and my 2 FREE mystery gifts (gifts are worth about $10). After receiving them, if I don't wish to receive any more books, I can return the shipping statement marked "cancel." If I don't cancel, I will receive 6 brand-new novels every month and be billed just $4.99 per book in the U.S. or $5.49 per book in Canada. That's a savings of at least 23% off the cover price. It's quite a bargain! Shipping and handling is just 50¢ per book in the U.S. and 75¢ per book in Canada.* I understand that accepting the 2 free books and gifts places me under no obligation to buy anything. I can always return a shipment and cancel at any time. Even if I never buy another book, the two free books and gifts are mine to keep forever.

122/322 IDN FVXH

Name	(PLEASE PRINT)	
Address		Apt. #
City	State/Prov.	Zip/Postal Code

Signature (if under 18, a parent or guardian must sign)

Mail to the **Reader Service:**
IN U.S.A.: P.O. Box 1867, Buffalo, NY 14240-1867
IN CANADA: P.O. Box 609, Fort Erie, Ontario L2A 5X3

**Are you a current subscriber to Love Inspired books
and want to receive the larger-print edition?
Call 1-800-873-8635 or visit www.ReaderService.com.**

* Terms and prices subject to change without notice. Prices do not include applicable taxes. Sales tax applicable in N.Y. Canadian residents will be charged applicable taxes. Offer not valid in Quebec. This offer is limited to one order per household. Not valid for current subscribers to Love Inspired Larger Print books. All orders subject to credit approval. Credit or debit balances in a customer's account(s) may be offset by any other outstanding balance owed by or to the customer. Please allow 4 to 6 weeks for delivery. Offer available while quantities last.

Your Privacy—The Reader Service is committed to protecting your privacy. Our Privacy Policy is available online at www.ReaderService.com or upon request from the Reader Service.

We make a portion of our mailing list available to reputable third parties that offer products we believe may interest you. If you prefer that we not exchange your name with third parties, or if you wish to clarify or modify your communication preferences, please visit us at www.ReaderService.com/consumerschoice or write to us at Reader Service Preference Service, P.O. Box 9062, Buffalo, NY 14269. Include your complete name and address.

LILPDIR12

REQUEST YOUR FREE BOOKS!
2 FREE RIVETING INSPIRATIONAL NOVELS
PLUS 2 FREE MYSTERY GIFTS

Love Inspired®
SUSPENSE

YES! Please send me 2 FREE Love Inspired® Suspense novels and my 2 FREE mystery gifts (gifts are worth about $10). After receiving them, if I don't wish to receive any more books, I can return the shipping statement marked "cancel." If I don't cancel, I will receive 4 brand-new novels every month and be billed just $4.49 per book in the U.S. or $4.99 per book in Canada. That's a savings of at least 22% off the cover price. It's quite a bargain! Shipping and handling is just 50¢ per book in the U.S. and 75¢ per book in Canada.* I understand that accepting the 2 free books and gifts places me under no obligation to buy anything. I can always return a shipment and cancel at any time. Even if I never buy another book, the two free books and gifts are mine to keep forever.

123/323 IDN FVXT

Name	(PLEASE PRINT)	
Address		Apt. #
City	State/Prov.	Zip/Postal Code

Signature (if under 18, a parent or guardian must sign)

Mail to the **Reader Service:**
IN U.S.A.: P.O. Box 1867, Buffalo, NY 14240-1867
IN CANADA: P.O. Box 609, Fort Erie, Ontario L2A 5X3

Are you a subscriber to Love Inspired Suspense
and want to receive the larger-print edition?
Call 1-800-873-8635 or visit www.ReaderService.com.

* Terms and prices subject to change without notice. Prices do not include applicable taxes. Sales tax applicable in N.Y. Canadian residents will be charged applicable taxes. Offer not valid in Quebec. This offer is limited to one order per household. Not valid for current subscribers to Love Inspired Suspense books. All orders subject to credit approval. Credit or debit balances in a customer's account(s) may be offset by any other outstanding balance owed by or to the customer. Please allow 4 to 6 weeks for delivery. Offer available while quantities last.

Your Privacy—The Reader Service is committed to protecting your privacy. Our Privacy Policy is available online at www.ReaderService.com or upon request from the Reader Service.

We make a portion of our mailing list available to reputable third parties that offer products we believe may interest you. If you prefer that we not exchange your name with third parties, or if you wish to clarify or modify your communication preferences, please visit us at www.ReaderService.com/consumerchoice or write to us at Reader Service Preference Service, P.O. Box 9062, Buffalo, NY 14269. Include your complete name and address.

LISDIR12R

REQUEST YOUR FREE BOOKS!

2 FREE INSPIRATIONAL NOVELS
PLUS 2
FREE
MYSTERY GIFTS

Love Inspired

HISTORICAL

INSPIRATIONAL HISTORICAL ROMANCE

YES! Please send me 2 FREE Love Inspired® Historical novels and my 2 FREE mystery gifts (gifts are worth about $10). After receiving them, if I don't wish to receive any more books, I can return the shipping statement marked "cancel." If I don't cancel, I will receive 4 brand-new novels every month and be billed just $4.49 per book in the U.S. or $4.99 per book in Canada. That's a savings of at least 22% off the cover price. It's quite a bargain! Shipping and handling is just 50¢ per book in the U.S. and 75¢ per book in Canada.* I understand that accepting the 2 free books and gifts places me under no obligation to buy anything. I can always return a shipment and cancel at any time. Even if I never buy another book, the two free books and gifts are mine to keep forever.

102/302 IDN FVYH

Name	(PLEASE PRINT)

Address		Apt. #

City	State/Prov.	Zip/Postal Code

Signature (if under 18, a parent or guardian must sign)

Mail to the **Reader Service:**
IN U.S.A.: P.O. Box 1867, Buffalo, NY 14240-1867
IN CANADA: P.O. Box 609, Fort Erie, Ontario L2A 5X3

Want to try two free books from another series?
Call 1-800-873-8635 or visit www.ReaderService.com.

---

* Terms and prices subject to change without notice. Prices do not include applicable taxes. Sales tax applicable in N.Y. Canadian residents will be charged applicable taxes. Offer not valid in Quebec. This offer is limited to one order per household. Not valid for current subscribers to Love Inspired Historical books. All orders subject to credit approval. Credit or debit balances in a customer's account(s) may be offset by any other outstanding balance owed by or to the customer. Please allow 4 to 6 weeks for delivery. Offer available while quantities last.

Your Privacy—The Reader Service is committed to protecting your privacy. Our Privacy Policy is available online at www.ReaderService.com or upon request from the Reader Service.

We make a portion of our mailing list available to reputable third parties that offer products we believe may interest you. If you prefer that we not exchange your name with third parties, or if you wish to clarify or modify your communication preferences, please visit us at www.ReaderService.com/consumerschoice or write to us at Reader Service Preference Service, P.O. Box 9062, Buffalo, NY 14269. Include your complete name and address.

LIHDIR12

Reader Service.com

Manage your account online!

- Review your order history
- Manage your payments
- Update your address

*We've designed
the Reader Service website
just for you.*

Enjoy all the features!

- Reader excerpts from any series
- Respond to mailings and special monthly offers
- Discover new series available to you
- Browse the Bonus Bucks catalogue
- Share your feedback

Visit us at:
ReaderService.com